L ROSE

PROTECTED

BY THE TIGER SHIFTER

Strawberrys.art

For the readers who would want to be stalked and kidnapped by a tiger shifter

BLURB

Nox

People see me as the asshole who deals with the hellish jobs. That's because people fear me, which is how I like it.

Unfortunately, I also have to put up with the tiger inside me. My beast should have protected me when I was younger, but instead, all he's ever wanted are pats and attention.

I've hated *that* tiger... until him.

Our fated mate.

Kieran

Single life as a young college professor with anxiety is trying. Add in my poor coordination and I often wonder

if there's someone in the world who will ever accept me as
I am.

Even the men my parents try to set me up with don't work
out—that second date never does come.

But after one heart-stopping, breathtaking glance from a
stranger, I figure that none of the men before him are
meant for me.

Thankfully, after a mugging and meeting a loveable tiger,
Nox is back in my life.

Now all I have to do is keep him there.

TRIGGER WARNINGS

Kidnapping and stalking

CHAPTER ONE

NOX

$\mathcal{A}$ few months ago, I turned into a stalker.

If that wasn't bad enough, I was now a kidnapper.

Fuck me and my damned days filled with following someone. But it was worth it. Or was it? It was. I scrubbed a hand over my face and strode from the knocked-out man on the couch in my office to hopefully find some sane help.

There, I admitted I needed it.

I should have asked for help months ago when I'd started creeping about.

No. Fuck that. I never should have turned to stalking in the goddamn first place. But I couldn't stop myself.

Not when *he* was my fated mate.

He was also the clumsiest, most oblivious man I'd ever

fucking seen, which made me and the tiger worry nonstop.

I knocked on my brother's door, and when I heard him call out, I opened it. "Can I speak with your mate?"

Rio sat up from Deacon's chest with wide eyes. "Me?"

Deacon flung the blanket on Rio, not wanting me to see his naked body, and barked, "Yes. Give him time."

I nodded, closing the door, and paced the hall while waiting.

Rio was the obvious choice to talk to since he was new and seemed more level-headed than Deacon, Riker, and me combined.

Besides, he wasn't a cold-blooded killer like my brothers and I were.

Even though his childhood had been shit, due to his cartel father who we recently murdered, his upbringing had still been less chaotic than ours.

Working for our shifter government on missions that pretty much gave us permission to kill helped to cool our desires to hunt and slaughter.

Truth be told, for my brothers, the hunger for blood comes more from Deacon's and Riker's animals than their human side. I'd just never told them it was my human side that wanted to murder those who deserved it, more than the animal instincts I held inside.

The tiger in me was a fucking timid little pussy.

I ground my teeth together when it purred inside me, trying to calm *me* down.

That was why I never shifted in front of anyone. If I did, the tiger would rather play or rub up against someone for attention. It never protected me when I was younger like my brothers' animals had.

The tiger had hid when there was trouble.

A *tiger*.

One of the meanest cats in the world wanted love and affection rather than to slaughter anyone who fucked us over.

The door opened.

Rio stared. "What's—"

"Come with me," I said quickly. Then I added tightly, almost reluctantly, "Please."

Rio nodded and followed me back to my office. I opened the door and moved aside. When Rio entered, I peeked out of the corner of my eye to see astonishment color his features.

He snapped his mouth closed and asked, "Nox, did you kidnap my professor?"

Yes.

Yes, I had.

I threw out a hand. "He's a danger to himself."

Rio hummed and nodded. "Right. And is that why you kidnapped him?"

"I'm surprised he's even alive. In the past months, he's nearly died thirty times." I glared down at my mate.

"O-kay," Rio drew out. "But why kidnap him because of it?"

I locked my teeth together, staring at *my* fated one. I softened a little when he made a noise and rubbed his cheek on the cushion, which made his glasses crooked.

He was cute.

Tiny but cute.

What the fuck was I going to do with him?

Rio sucked in a breath. "He's your mate."

I dragged my gaze away from Kieran Higgins and looked to Rio, nodding once.

"Holy shit." He covered his mouth with his hand, and behind it he said, "And you kidnapped him."

"Can we focus on something else?" I snarled.

"No, Nox. We can't." Now he was the one pacing. "Let me get this straight. You've been watching him awhile. Well, you must've been because you said in the last few months he's nearly died—" A growl rolled out of me. Rio rolled his eyes. "Yes, okay, I won't mention that *D* word again. Then you decided to... take him to protect him from himself?" He stopped pacing and looked at me.

Sighing, I nodded.

"Nox," he groaned, as if in pain.

How was he in pain? He hadn't watched my mate for the past few months while he nearly lost his life from tripping or being too absorbed in reading or his phone to realize he could have been run over, squashed, or *murdered*.

Anger and fear stabbed me in the chest.

"Can't I keep him here, so he stays safe?" I asked.

Rio spluttered before he thinned his lips and drew his brows together.

Fucking Christ.

Logically, I knew I couldn't keep him, but when I saw those men pull him into an alley, mug him, and then knock him out, I couldn't leave my mate out in the world for something else to happen.

Fury clawed at my throat.

They were going to do things to him.

Bad, bad fucking things.

Things I couldn't think about because I'd want to—

"You can't keep him."

My upper lip rose in a silent snarl.

"Don't get angry at me. You obviously didn't think this over. He's your fated mate, Nox. Get to know him. Woo him. I'm sure you'll win him over and then he'll never want to leave your side."

"I don't fucking woo."

"All right, can you at least be nice? Less snarly and grumpy?"

Crossing my arms over my chest, I scowled at my brother's mate. Maybe he wasn't the right choice to bring in here. At least Deacon and Riker would be on board with my idea of kidnapping and keeping him here.

Rio pinched the bridge of his nose. "Nox." He sighed again. "What made you kidnap him today? What was the underlying cause, since it seems he's accident prone anyway?"

"He had his nose stuck in a damn book once again and two men took him into a darkened alley. He didn't even yell for assistance. Before I crossed the road to help, they'd stolen his wallet and knocked him out. I brought him back here."

"Uh-huh." He nodded. "And what happened to the muggers?"

I had a feeling he didn't want me to say I killed them.

Still....

"I killed them."

"Nox," he snapped. "Did anyone see you? Are the

bodies just lying in the alleyway with the professor's wallet?"

I cocked a brow.

He ran a hand through his hair. "Right. Of course you would clean up after yourself, considering your job."

"They were going to...." My blood boiled. I stretched my neck from side to side to try and cool myself down and stop myself from hunting for more blood. "They wanted to do other things to him when he was passed out."

Rio paled as he nodded. "How do you know?"

I grinned. Rio took the slightest step away. I rolled my eyes. I would never hurt him, but my smile could have come across as a little crazed from remembering the way they'd cried and begged. "I tortured them for answers. It didn't last anywhere near long enough, and I couldn't make it too bloody, since I didn't want to get any on me in case it got on him."

"Right. Yes. Of course."

"Exactly. Now, what do I do about—"

We froze and stared at my mate when he moaned and shifted on the couch.

Please don't wake. Please don't wake, I mentally begged.

Rio waved his hand at me. I looked there to see him pointing at me and then my mate. I shook my head. I was not talking to him. I couldn't. I wouldn't risk the bond forming more. He had a chance at a better life. A life without the knowledge that monsters were real.

I shook my head.

Rio nodded.

I shook my head again and pointed at him then my mate.

He glared and mouthed, "No."

Another moan from my mate, and he pulled an arm up to rub over his face, knocking his glasses to the side.

Shit, fuck.

Panic had me shifting from human to tiger in a matter of moments.

"Nox, no," Rio barked low.

A groan from my mate, but before I ran to hide behind a desk, he slowly sat up.

"Fuck you, No—"

"Mr. Santiago?"

"Oh, ah, hey, Professor Higgins."

Getting down on our belly, we peeked out from under the desk. Our mate blinked in a confused daze up at Rio.

"W-What... where am I?"

Rio clasped his hands behind his back. "Well, you see... what do you remember?"

We thought that was a good question. Maybe the bear's mate wasn't so bad after all.

Digging our claws into the carpet, I fought for dominance in this form, easily winning since all the tiger wanted to do was to scent mark our mate. But now I was at the forefront of the brain, it left me in control of this form.

"Um..." His brows dip. "I was walking home from college and—" He gasped. "—two men dragged me into an alley and took my wallet. They knocked me out. I have to call the police. Do you have a phone?"

"I... don't?"

He was useless at lying.

My mate straightened, but then rubbed at his head and wincing. "You don't have a phone?"

"No," Rio drew out.

They both looked to the desk at the same time where a phone sat.

Fuck.

He couldn't call the cops.

Besides, I had his wallet.

Which was in my clothes on the floor where I'd shifted.

Jesus Christ.

My mate stood, but Rio got in his way, yelling, "Wait—"

"I don't have time for this—" he broke off on a cry and jolted back where he then tripped and fell onto the couch again. "Mr. Santiago," he screamed. "Tiger! There's a tiger!"

Shit, my control had slipped, and I'd let the tiger sit up. It placed its paws on the desk to jump on top of it but quickly dropped back onto the floor on the other side.

No, I mentally command.

Yet, I wouldn't mind knowing the answer to what the tiger wanted to find out. That if our mate wanted to pat it, feel its fur in a long, loving stroke.

"Mr. Santiago!" He looked frantically at the only other human in the room.

"It's, ah, okay?" Rio tried.

"It does not look okay, Mr. Santiago. Is this your pet—"

A snarl erupted out of me. We were no one's pet... except maybe his.

No. I wouldn't allow that.

Pushing back into control, I went down to my belly and let the purr the tiger wanted to share out. Our mate slowly looked back to us.

I crept closer and noticed how our mate stilled.

"Aww, isn't he adorable," Rio cooed. If he wasn't trying to help our mate relax, I would have ripped his head off. "He's trying to look less intimidating to calm you."

"Before he eats me?"

"No," Rio said quickly. "He, ah, wants pats."

I wanted to turn and growl, maybe even attack Rio for even suggesting it, but I couldn't look away from my mate when the tension rolled off him as he relaxed his shoulders.

"Really?" he asked hopefully.

Fuck my life, was I really going to let him pat me?

Shit. Yes, I was.

I got us to our feet and sniffed at our mate. His sweet, delicious scent had us closing our eyes, and we purred louder while we rubbed our head against his knees.

A laugh escaped him. "This is amazing."

"I know," Rio replied.

He better not tell my brothers about this.

My mate's hands shook as he reached out slowly. We pushed our head up and under his palms and we purred some more when his fingers threaded through our fur to then run over our head.

"I can't believe this," my mate said in awe.

Pleasure had us licking and tasting our mate's skin on

his arms. The tiger liked hearing the praise from our mate. And hell, I didn't mind knowing he thought the tiger was likeable.

His arms wrapped around our neck and hugged us close.

We tipped back and licked over his face, drawing out a laugh.

He stilled and placed his attention on Rio. Thankfully, he went back to rubbing our body while he asked, "Are you even allowed a pet tiger?"

A grumbled growl rolled out.

Again, we were no one's pet.

Except his... maybe.

Fuck. I was kidding myself if I tried to deny my attraction to our mate.

We wanted him.

No, *I* wanted him.

But he deserved a world of ignorance. Without the fear of the monsters in the world.

There're monsters in humans as well.

Kieran nearly lost his life because of them.

"Ah, yes?" Rio lied pitifully. "He's an exception."

"Wow, I wish I could get one."

Growling again, we placed our front paws on the couch. My mate leaned away, shock evident with his gaping mouth.

We touched our nose to his and continued growling.

He was to never get another tiger. They wouldn't be like us, and knowing his luck, he would get eaten by it.

"Mr. Santiago?" my mate called, worry tightening his tone.

"It's okay. He just doesn't want you to mention other tigers."

There was a pause, and I wondered how Rio was going to explain this away.

"Oh, okay." My mate beamed up at us and cupped our cheeks. Jesus, he *would* get killed by any other tiger. "I won't. You're all I need."

Hearing those words was like a slap in the face to wake me the fuck up, but they also lit my gut alight with fireflies.

I was all he needed.

No, *we* were all he needed.

He'd said that.

Back to purring, we rubbed our face against his. Over his head, his chest, his waist.

There was a deep desire taking over to have all of him smelling like us. Then once he did, maybe the stab of possessiveness would fade.

Hopefully.

Although currently, *I* was still considering keeping him here in one way or another, and I wasn't opposed to tying him to my bed.

CHAPTER TWO

Thank God I didn't embarrass myself when I spotted the ginormous, sharp-toothed tiger, who was currently pulling his hind legs up onto the couch to join the rest of him and me. My heart danced over a few extra beats when he lay down with a groan and rested his head on my lap. His purr was such a soothing sound. One I wanted to fall asleep to.

I still couldn't wrap my head around the fact I was in the presence of an actual tiger. My pulse hadn't slowed yet and I doubted it would any time soon. Though, who would have thought such a predator would rest on the couch with someone like a house cat wanting pets.

He was an absolute stunner. His orange, black, and white coat was softer than I thought it would be. His golden eyes were almost mesmerizing. I could confess that his teeth were still a little scary, but I was confident he wouldn't kill me. Yet, I was only going off Mr. Santiago's relaxed state. It wasn't like I was going to ignore the chance to get up close and personal with a tiger either.

His wet, warm, rough tongue lolled out and swiped at my arm.

I didn't mind the slobber he left behind. How could I when he was so amazing. Plus, he liked me enough to relax around me. Then again, I wasn't intimidating at all.

Pushing my glasses up my nose, I glided my hand over his head and neck.

"How did you get him?" I asked.

"The pet store?" What Mr. Santiago, an ex-student at the college I worked at, said sounded more like a question than an answer. The tiger huffed out a hot breath.

Looking up, I shook my head. "I don't think you can get a tiger at a pet store, Mr. Santiago."

"Rio, please."

I nodded. "Rio, and since I'm not your professor any longer, you can call me Kieran."

"Thanks. How's college?"

Shaking my head, I ignored that question to ask my own, "I know I was distracted by the tiger, but I'd really like for you to tell me how I got here and why you won't give me the phone?"

Rio opened and closed his mouth. I could see his mind tick over through his darting gaze.

Why couldn't he just tell me the truth?

It didn't make sense.

"Well, you see... I happened along the alleyway after

you got knocked out and I told those guys off. When they ran away, I brought you back here."

I wasn't buying it at all.

Anxiety had my stomach twisting.

Something was going on here. Why was he lying to me? What was the point?

"Why didn't you take me to the hospital or call the police yourself?"

"I wasn't thinking after chasing those guys off. For some reason, I thought you'd be safer here."

"Do you have my wallet then?"

I jumped when the tiger suddenly got off the couch and went to... a pile of clothes on the floor. He scratched and clawed at them. Rio went over and picked up the pants, pulling my wallet free.

"That's mine," I announced, like he didn't know already. But maybe he didn't because he was staring at it like it surprised him.

"Right." He nodded and came over to hand it to me.

"Why was it on the floor in a pocket?" I asked.

Rio tensed. "Because... I got changed when I got home."

I blinked slowly. "Excuse me?"

He rubbed at the back of his neck. "I wanted to get out of those clothes when I got home."

"Here? In the room while I was passed out on the couch?"

Rio cringed. "It wasn't creepy or anything."

This was strange. Way too strange for me.

A subject change was needed, and I couldn't help but

say what was still on my mind. "I probably should call the police. Those men could do it to someone else."

"No!" Rio yelled and then laughed awkwardly. "I mean, what's the point? I ran them off and they didn't get your wallet in the end anyway. I'm sure they won't do it again."

"But I was attacked."

"And you're fine," Rio tried. The tiger swiped at him, but Rio jumped back quickly before the tiger stalked back over to me and sat at my feet, facing Rio.

"I... I suppose I could leave it since I don't really remember what they look like." Which was a pity because I would go to the police if I did. I didn't want anyone else to get hurt.

Rio clicked his fingers and pointed at me. "See, no reason to annoy the police."

I hummed under my breath as a new question popped up. "Rio?" It was a question that had been burning in my mind since I last saw him.

"Yeah?"

"That, um, man you were with in class. The day you left and didn't return."

"Oh yeah, I quit. I never wanted to have a business degree in the first place. I was more forced into it. But anyway, why are you asking about Nox?"

Nox

"Nox," I whispered, wanting to test the name out. I scraped my teeth over my bottom lip. Nerves suddenly locked my words in. The thought of the bulky, built man with some tattooed patterns on the back of his neck, which I was sure ran down over his muscled back, had given me constant butterflies. I'd never wished before to have the chance to run my fingers through someone's hair, until that day in the lecture room when my fingers had twitched at the thought of how soft his light brown hair was. I could picture it easily now. How it was short at the sides and longer on top. Similar to mine, except mine was a bit longer and black.

My thoughts fled when I felt the tiger's body tense under my hands.

Rio nodded. "Nox, he's my—"

"What?" I demanded and knew my cheeks reddened.

Rio's lips twitched. "Brother-in-law."

Rio was going to laugh at me now. It happened a lot, though that was mainly over my lack of coordination. Still, I needed to know who the man was. From one brief glance of his gold-colored irises that had my heart leaping, I couldn't get him off my mind. Only on that day, I'd quickly looked away from Nox. I'd been burned by good-looking men before. Some of them had even grown agitated if I stared too long.

I wasn't a handsome man. Too skinny, too short, too smart, too shy, and awkward.

My reserved nature, plus my average looks, made it hard to get a date or to keep one for a second chance. I tended to fumble things I held and trip over nothing most of the time.

Immediately, I regretted showing my interest in Nox.

I hoped Rio wouldn't say anything to his brother-in-law. I'd just been curious.

Hold on....

Shock had me blurting, "Wait, you said brother-in-law. Are you married?" Rio was younger than I was.

Rio chuckled. "I am. Deacon is amazing. If you stick around long enough, you might get to meet him. And it was Deacon who sent Nox to college to guard me. He's very protective."

I wasn't sure if my staying was a good idea since, from the glance to the clock on the wall, I saw it was already late, and I still had papers to grade. Then again, I couldn't seem to bring myself to stand from the couch. It meant I would have to leave this amazing creature in front of me.

Nodding, I leaned forward to run my hands over the tiger's back.

"What's his name?" I asked, trying to change the subject.

"Ah... Fluffy?"

"Fluffy?"

He coughed, but I was sure I heard a laugh behind it too. "Yes."

Blood pumped faster when the tiger pulled his upper lip back and snarled toward Rio. At least it wasn't aimed at me. He didn't like being called Fluffy at all. *Poor guy.*

"Are you sure it's legal to keep a tiger in captivity?"

"I'm sure. Deacon told me all about it. Fluffy is too... hmm, how should I put it... gentle? Soft? He wouldn't survive in the wilderness on his own."

Fluffy snarled again, but Rio ignored the viciousness like it was an everyday occurrence. Heck, maybe it was.

"Well, he sounds scary," I said, hugging him to me. "You could easily intimidate other animals," I told Fluffy as I rubbed my face into his soft fur. A purr started from within him, making me grin. After a few moments, I reluctantly straightened, fixed my glasses, and massaged my fingers into the tiger's neck.

His purr grew louder and my smile grew so wide, my cheeks hurt.

Until he suddenly stood and growled at the door. Slowly, I pulled my hands from him.

Rio's eyes widened.

"What's wrong?" I asked.

Rio forced a laugh and went to the door, leaning against it. "Nothing. Nothing at all."

A knock sounded. The doorhandle jiggled.

"Nox, you've got something against the door."

Hold up, I was in Nox's office? My pulse kicked up, and embarrassingly, my dick jerked under my pants. I wasn't a teen. My body didn't need to react in such a manner just from being in someone's room.

Actually, it had never reacted like that in the past, even if I'd entered my crush's domain.

Why was it now?

"Nox isn't here right now," Rio called. "Come back later, Riker."

The tiger slowly and quietly crept behind the couch to hide.

Maybe he wouldn't survive in the wild if he was worried about another person.

"Ooooh, are you and Deacon doing it in there? Nox will kill you," the man named Riker called.

"Holy shit, Riker. Deacon and I do have standards."

"Do you? Really? I could scent you guys in the movie—"

"Shut up," Rio yelled.

Scent?

What?

"Riker, I have a guest in here. My professor. Can you give me a second?"

"Does my brother know about this guest?"

"Yes?"

That sounded like a lie.

Standing, I pressed a hand to my unsettled stomach. "Rio, I can leave if—"

The tiger snarled as he ran around the front of the couch to stand in my way.

"No, no," Rio said. "Everything is—Fuck you, Riker," Rio yelled as he got pushed our way by an arm sticking through the gap before the door swung open.

A short and slim man like me, but with more muscles, bright orange hair, and amber eyes, stared into the room with a gaping mouth.

"Nox—"

"Fluffy," Rio shouted, causing me to jump. "That's our pet tiger, Fluffy, Riker." He stomped over to Riker and grabbed his arm.

"Right," Riker drew out. "And that's your professor?"

"Yes. Kieran, this is my husband's other brother, Riker."

Riker's big grin and shining eyes put me on edge. In fact, the hairs on the back of my neck rose.

"Hello," I offered, pushing my glasses up my nose.

"Hey. Hi. Nice to meet you. Though, I'm not sure why I'm meeting you. What're you doing in our house? Did Rio really invite you? I can't believe he did because

Deacon wouldn't like that... unless Rio wants you dead." He turned to Rio. "Do you want him dead? I can do it if—"

Rio's hand slapped over Riker's mouth.

My nerves rattled around inside me, and I had the biggest urge to steal the tiger while running for my life.

"No one is killing anyone, Riker."

That actually sounded like Riker had really meant his offer of killing me.

I took a step back and the tiger followed.

Riker took Rio's wrist and pulled his hand away from his mouth. "Boo. That's boring. Then what's he doing here?"

"He's here because I saved him from a mugging and.... You know what? It doesn't matter why he's here. Can you do me a favor and take Fluffy out to, ah, go potty and see if you can find Nox? I need him here, *right now*, to take the professor home."

"Nox will take me home?" I blurted, and Riker's eyes narrowed on me.

Until his brows shot up when his eyes widened. "No way. He's—"

"Riker. Fluffy. Now!" Rio yelled. He seemed super stressed. He looked to the tiger. "Fluffy, go." He pointed toward the door.

Fluffy took a step that way, glanced back at me, and walked close so he could brush his face into my side.

Reaching out, I patted his head when he paused in front of me, waiting for the attention. His height was unbelievable. The top of his ears was up to my chest. He was the biggest tiger I'd ever seen. Then again, I didn't get up close and personal with the ones at the zoo.

"It's okay," I told him. "I'll come back to visit." He started purring as I met Rio's gaze. "I can visit him, right?"

My face heated. It was rude of me to ask to see a tiger over the owners of the house.

Quickly, I added, "Not that... I mean, I would like to drop by for... would you...." *Oh God, please let the floor open to swallow me whole.* "I know I was your professor but... coffee? Maybe?"

Rio's lips twitched while Riker chuckled and winked. "I like you."

Fluffy growled and stopped licking my arm so he could turn to swipe his paw out toward Riker's way.

Rio pinched the bridge of his nose and sighed. "Riker, please take Fluffy out."

"I don't think Fluffy wants to go with him," I said gently, trying not to offend the man who spoke of murder.

"He will." Riker grinned. He crouched and tapped his thighs. "Come on, Fluffy. Be a good boy and I'll give you some catnip."

Fluffy huffed and turned his back on Riker to gaze up at me.

Riker scowled. "If you don't come here, I'll tell—" His grin was back in full force when Fluffy suddenly bounded over to him.

Laughing, I wiped away the slobber on my arms as I watched him leave. But just before Riker closed the door after them, Fluffy turned back my way. My chest warmed that the tiger didn't want to leave me, and my gut tightened, seeing him go.

Maybe I needed a pet of my own.

"Kieran," Rio called, and when I met his gaze, he added, "You can drop by anytime you want to visit Fluffy. I'm sure he'd love it."

Smiling, I dipped my head. "Thank you." Already, I couldn't wait to see him next. However, the excited thrill that ran up my spine wasn't about visiting the tiger. Instead, it was for who I was about to see and who would be taking me home.

CHAPTER THREE

NOX

Once I was in my bedroom, I shifted into my human form. Bones cracked and reformed, fur disappeared, teeth reshaped, and sharp claws shortened, all while I silently cursed the tiger for popping onto the desk in the first place for our mate to see us. Now the man would expect goddamn Fluffy to be in the house whenever he dropped by. Yet, no matter what I called the animal, he didn't give a shit. Instead, he was lounging happily after receiving so much attention from our fated.

"So," Riker drew out from where he stood, leaning against the wall just inside the door.

I ignored him and got dressed into black jeans and shirt.

Riker growled under his breath. "You're not going to say anything?"

I went to my bedside table and grabbed some socks to put on.

"Nox," my brother whined. "Just tell me for certain. He's your fated, right? He's your one? Which means I really can have one out there. I mean, it can't just happen to Deacon and you, then not me, right? The world can't be that cruel.... Fuck, yes it can."

Shit.

I didn't want him upset. I fucking hated seeing either of my brothers hurt.

After slipping my boots on, I turned, walked over, and gripped his shoulder. When his gaze shot to mine, I said, "He is my fated mate, and I believe you will receive one too."

The way his face lit up was worth saying it, and now I prayed it wasn't a fucking lie. Riker deserved one over me. He had a softness to him that needed protecting... to keep him from going off the rails.

"Do you like yours?" he whispered.

Closing my eyes, I tightened my hold on his shoulder as the image of my fated conjured instantly.

He was shorter, but in the perfect kind of way where I could pick him up and carry him around. He wore glasses, but the sexy kind, and they worked well for his hot nerdy look.... What in the fuck was I thinking?

Opening my eyes, I clenched my jaw. He was soft, kind, sweet, and smart.

Better than I could ever amount to be. He needed someone who was like him and not the complete opposite.

"I like mine enough to keep away from him."

At least, I think I could.

Maybe.

For him I wanted to.

It was a good idea.

Riker shook his head. "Can I tell you something, Nox?"

Drawing my brows together, I nodded.

"You're a fucking moron." He shoved at my chest. "Stop thinking about yourself and think about your mate. He was picked for you. Maybe *he* needs you and only you can make *him* happy. Stop thinking of your damn self and think of your mate. Do you know what his life is like? Maybe he was brought to you for protection."

Breathing unsteadily, I shook my head.

"Would you really leave your mate alone? Will he ever find love? He'd be miserable. On his own to fend for himself. If you don't accept him first, you're leaving him without a choice of a life where *you* could make him happy and safe. Fate did well for Deacon. They have for you, too, but you're just being a stubborn dickhead."

If I didn't claim him, would he have someone else?

Someone who would make him happy?

Someone who would love him?

Touch him?

Fuck him?

Bite him?

My teeth elongated, and I ran my tongue over them while a rumbled growl rolled out. "No one else gets to touch him. Make him happy. He's mine."

Riker grinned. "He is."

I glanced to the door and back to Riker. I willed my teeth back to their normal size. "What do I do with him?"

My brother cackled as he moved from one foot to another. "Care the hell out of him. Show him you're worth it. Let him see the real you. Woo him. Taste him. Sink inside him. Bite him. Lick his blood from your lips. Fuck him. C—"

"I get it," I snarled in his face.

He laughed again and patted my arm. "If you don't like hearing me talk about him like that, then get your stupid ass in there and get to work." He bounced from toes to heel and clasped his hand in front of him. "This is so cool. I love this for you. By the way, your tiger is adorable. I tried to remember the last time I saw him, but we would've been cubs."

Reaching up, I rested my hand on his head and ruffled his damn hair. "Thanks for talking some sense into me." I ignored the compliment and comment about the tiger because I didn't want to talk about him at all. The thing was too weak.

"Anytime. I can hit you next time to knock logic into you," he offered.

I smirked. "I'll let you know if I need it."

He huffed out a laugh. "Oh, you'll need it. Go talk to your fated, and when you get home later, you can tell me how you saved him from muggers." I raised a brow and Riker snorted. "Rio is a good cook, but a shit liar."

Huffing, I nodded and opened my door.

My body went out of control—heart, pulse, mind, gut, and dick—from the thought of being in *his* presence again. It wasn't only my body, but the tiger constantly purred in my head.

Wiping my hands on my jeans, I turned the handle to my office and pushed it open.

"Here he is," Rio announced.

My gaze went straight to *him*.

My mate stood where I'd left him, on the other side of the office. He pushed his glasses up his nose while he puffed out a breath.

Rio cleared his throat. "Nox, this is, ah, our professor, well, my ex-professor because you were only there to.... Fuck it. Nox, Kieran. Kieran Higgins, this is Nox Blackwood, my brother-in-law, and he'll be taking you home because no doubt my husband will be down those stairs shortly looking for me."

That was an obvious hint from Rio for us to leave before Deacon saw this and asked too many questions. I wasn't ready for the third degree in front of my mate.

But... what did I say to my fated for the first time?

Red touched his cheeks, and he lifted a hand to wave quickly. "Hi."

Grunting, I tipped my chin up at him.

His lips thinned and his gaze dulled a little before it fell from me to the floor while his blush spread.

Had I upset him?

A foot to my shin had my eyes snapping to Rio. He was lucky he was my brother's fated or else I would have snapped his neck for that. Rio nodded toward my mate and mouthed, "Talk."

Shit.

Okay, I could do nice.

For him.

What was nice?

Fuck.

"I...." Grinding my teeth together, I narrowed my gaze in annoyance when my brain picked that moment to stop functioning. My mate glanced my way, saw my frustrated scowl, and I knew he thought it was directed at him when he quickly looked back to the floor. His heart hammered under his ribs in fear, and scenting that pissed me the fuck off. I never wanted him to be scared of me.

Out of the corner of my eye, I caught Rio pulling back his leg. I dodged his kick with a sidestep. My action brought my mate's attention to me, and I waved a hand toward the door. "*Please*, follow me."

He opened his mouth, closed it, and swallowed thickly, but managed to nod my way before saying to Rio, "Thank you for helping me."

"No problem at all. I'm sure I'll see you another time or else Fluffy will miss you." Rio gave him a pat on the shoulder as he passed, which had my mate stumbling forward a little. I reached out and steadied him with my hands to his arms and glared over his head at Rio, who backed up a step with his hands out in front of him.

"Sorry," Rio called.

My mate let out a shy laugh. "It's okay. My coordination isn't the best." He flicked his gaze up to me and away again. "Sorry."

It was on the tip of my tongue to say, "You should be since I worry about you all the fucking time." But I refrained and instead said, "You don't need to apologize."

The lie was worth it because he lifted his head and smiled up at me.

I stared at it. His lips. The smile slipped and I knew it was because of my attention to it.

Fuck.

With a hand to his back, which caused my mate to shiver, my hand to tingle and gut to swoosh, I led him out the door. I briefly glanced over my shoulder and offered Rio a chin lift in thanks. He grinned and gave me a thumbs-up.

By the time we made it to the garage and got into my car, my mate had managed to trip twice over nothing. The clumsiness made me fist the back of his shirt to hold him upright. He'd blushed and mumbled more apologies, but I brushed them off, even though worry ate at my organs.

How had he lived without killing himself so far?

"Address... please?"

I already knew where he lived. I'd been his stalker after all. But he didn't know that. When he told me, I reversed the car out, turned it around, and drove off.

"Do you know that area?" he asked softly. God, I loved his sweet voice. At least it was directed at me this time instead of me hearing it while being hidden. It left me eager to discover what he would sound like in bed.

"Yes," I said sharply, but only because I was thinking of being inside him.

"Okay." I could hear the dejection in his tone from my clipped response.

Fuck me. I wanted to shoot myself in the head.

Strangling the wheel instead, I glanced at him, and he stared out the window with a frown.

I'd put that on his lips.

He should have been smiling.

He should always smile.

I liked when he did. When I'd witnessed them from my hiding spots.

A phone chimed.

My mate looked to the center console where his phone sat. His brows pinched as he picked up the device. "This is mine."

Grunting, I shrugged. "Rio takes my car sometimes. Guess he picked you up in it."

"How do you know—"

"Riker. And I watched Rio enter the house with you from within my other office."

Christ, I hated lying, but he wasn't ready to hear the truth. *I'm a stalking murderer who wants to put his prick in you and claim you so you can never leave.*

I also kidnapped you and was so close to keeping you locked up.

Though, the urge to see him restrained hadn't subsided yet.

He nodded, accepting what I said, and unlocked his phone to read the message.

"Shit," he mumbled, and probably thought I wouldn't hear it, but being a shifter, I had.

"You seem tense. Is everything okay?"

Holy fuck, I wanted to pat myself on the back since I managed a full sentence, even when my nerves were punching me in the gut.

His warm smile made my efforts worth it. Though, it really wasn't an effort since it was for my mate. I already knew I'd do anything to make him feel at ease around me.

Slip-ups were bound to happen, and then I'd have to kick myself in the balls whenever I made him upset.

"You're very perceptive." He waved his phone. "It's just my parents being annoying."

"You have parents?" I hadn't seen him visit them in the last few months.

A sweet soft laugh escaped him, until he covered his mouth with his hand. "Sorry, I didn't mean to laugh at what you said, but doesn't everyone have parents in some form or another? Well, at least at one point in time."

I hummed.

He quickly rushed on with "Anyway, it's fine. They think since I'm twenty-seven, I should already be engaged or married off. They like to help me by setting me up on dates. They've sent me a new possible candidate.... Are you okay?"

Glancing at him, I saw his worried gaze was on my hands that were clenching and unclenching around the wheel while I visualized them wrapped around this new guy's neck. I liked that his parents cared, but I was on the scene now. They needed to back off.

Maybe I could have a chat with them.

Or *I* could take my mate on a date, state my intentions, and then he'd let them know he didn't need anyone else.

"I'm fine. Good. Would you like to go to eat somewhere?" I stared out the windscreen unblinking as I heard his sharp intake of breath.

"Me?" he choked, flushing with heat.

While my heart readjusted from my throat back down to where it belonged, I nodded. "Yeah."

"Oh, um, I... sure. Please. Food would be good."

The corner of my mouth ticked up. Even the tiger was pleased, knowing we were feeding our mate. "All right. Are you allergic to anything?"

"Peanuts."

Of course he was.

"Burgers? I know a place."

"I could eat a burger." He placed his phone between his legs and rubbed his hands up and down his thighs. "I guess it is dinner time anyway, right?"

"It is."

He wiped at a spot on his pants. "I'm a little dirty, probably from the mugging."

My heart jumped over an extra beat. My mate was worried about how he looked; I could tell by the way he was now trying to straighten his clothes out.

"You look nice," I told him and cringed at myself. I wasn't sure if "nice" sounded good enough to put him at ease.

But I guessed it was when he stopped fussing and relaxed back into the seat. "Thanks."

I hummed in return and drove into the parking area of the small diner I liked. Stopping, I turned off the car and climbed out. I caught through the window my mate quickly getting his seat belt off, opening the door, and stumbling out before I could even get there.

I'd been planning to grab the door for him. Maybe he was worried I'd leave him behind.

Sadness tightened my chest.

I wouldn't leave him.

Even if he never wanted to see me again, I'd always make sure he was safe.

"I'm ready," he announced, brushing himself off.

"I was going to get your door."

His brows shot up. "You were?"

"Yeah." Before I could drag him into a hug, I about-faced and walked toward the diner. Thankfully, I heard him follow me. At the entrance, I yanked the door open and stepped back.

He grinned up at me like I hung the moon and stars.

He deserved a blow job filled with so much pleasure he would see stars.

"Thank you." He suddenly stopped and paled. "I'm gay," he blurted. "I-I just thought you should know because... well, I know you don't frown upon sexuality seeing as your brother... but.... Forget it. Sorry." He rushed through the door and over to a free booth toward the back.

Was my mate trying to warn me?

Fuck me, I wanted to laugh.

He hadn't needed to since I was set on this being our first date.

Shit. He hasn't caught on that this is a date.

I made my way over to where he sat, covering his face with his menu, and took the opposite seat. I'd have liked to have been sitting next to him, but I didn't want to crowd him. Yet.

"It doesn't matter you prefer men, mate."

Shove a gag in my mouth. I fucked up and called him—

He peeked over the top of the menu. "Mate? Are you originally from Australia?"

No. Mate means we're connected in a way where I never want you gone.

Will you want me as well?

He had asked about me to Rio, which could mean I had a chance.

"Yes," I lied.

"Oh, I didn't know." He laughed lightly. "Of course I didn't know. Duh." He blushed, hiding once again. When his phone chimed, he placed the menu down and pulled it from his pocket. A frown appeared as he read the message.

"Parents?" I asked.

He nodded. "They're great. They are. But they don't understand that the men they set me up with just aren't interested after—Oh God, please ignore me. I don't know why I said that."

He went to pick up the menu again, but I reached out and touched my hand to his, stilling him.

He stared down at our hands as his breathing increased.

I licked my dry lips and ignored the voice in my head telling me I was making the wrong choice by saying something so soon.

Opening my mouth, I stalled over saying his name for the first time.

Kieran.

Kieran Higgins.

If he would have me, I would do everything in my power to let him know he was precious.

"Kieran," I said softly, and his eyes flew up to mine. "Tell your parents you're already on a date."

He jolted a little, asking, "I am?"

My lips twitched. "Yeah."

"With you?"

I brushed my thumb over the top of his hand, and he shivered. We loved that reaction from him. "I should've made it clear when I mentioned eating that I'd like for you to see this as a date."

Fuck me. Did I say that okay? Why couldn't I just tell him we were on a date and that was final. No questions.

"Um... okay... thank you."

Christ, he was cute, and sexy, and mine.

The tiger inside purred. He wanted out to rub up against Kieran again since our scent was weakening on him.

Kieran. I wanted to say his name all the time now.

Smiling, I tilted my head to the side. "You're thanking me for taking you out to dinner?"

His blush deepened. "I think so."

Shaking my head, I tipped my chin his way. "Figure out what you want to eat, and I'll go order while you text your parents."

"You got it" was his enthusiastic reply before he picked up his menu again.

The happiness on his face had me swimming in pride.

I wasn't sure how I got lucky that Kieran agreed this was a date, but I'd take that luck and pray it'd stick with me for the rest of my time with him tonight... until I dropped him off home.

I'd have to leave him then.

Fuck that. I wasn't leaving him where he could get hurt or worse.

Asking for a sleepover would be too much, too soon, but it didn't mean I couldn't watch from afar.

My brothers would probably tell me I was being stupid for not wanting to leave him. Then again, I was talking about Deacon who organized guards to follow Rio everywhere he went when outside the house and away from him.

CHAPTER FOUR

KIERAN

*A*fter I gave Nox my order and he refused my money, I watched him walk up to the counter. He wanted to pay for my meal too. I bit down on my bottom lip, so my mouth didn't drop open in shock. None of the other dates before him had. They'd all wanted to split the bill.

Nox had also seen me being clumsy and was still sticking around.

I wanted to believe those were all good signs.

My body certainly wanted to as well. The man turned my stomach into a ball of nervous excitement with a sprinkle of lust that had my cock half hard.

Smiling, I dragged my gaze away from him down on the table.

"Shit," I muttered, picking up my phone since I was

supposed to be messaging my parents that *I was on a date.* I gnawed on my bottom lip again to keep the squeal inside.

KIERAN:

> Mom, whoever you planned for me to dine with tomorrow at your place, please cancel them.

MOM:

> Honey, he's such a nice boy, and his mom said that he needs a pick me up after his last relationship.

DAD:

> Son, listen to your mom. Besides, the last time we saw you was when you got back from your holiday and that was MONTHS ago.

MOM:

> Exactly. Do you not love us? Just try this guy on when you're here to catch up with us.

DAD:

> Try this guy on, Babs? Is our son going to carve this banker's skin off and wear it?

KIERAN:

I don't need that visual, Dad.

DAD:

Me either. It's your mom we gotta worry about. One day she'll carve me up and wear me.

MOM:

All jokes aside (which aren't funny anyway) tell us you're coming to dinner.

KIERAN:

I'll come to dinner IF you cancel on that guy because I'm already on a date!!!!! I don't want to jinx it, but things are going well.

MOM:

OMG!!! Praise the lord. Will you bring him to dinner?

KIERAN:

Mom, this is our first date. I'm not scaring him off by asking him to meet my parents.

DAD:

We'll see you both tomorrow.

KIERAN:

No!

MOM:

See you at six. Kisses!!!!!!!

KIERAN:

I'll be there, but there'll be no one else with me. Which means you don't need to cook for a billion people, Mom.

DAD:

Forgot to say, if the date goes reeeaaalllly well, wrap it before you tap it.

I palmed my face and glanced over to see Nox walking back with two sodas.

DAD:

Wait, does that work for you? You don't need to wrap it if you're getting it, right? Tell the guy to wrap it.

Oh my God. My parents were weird.

KIERAN:

I'm going.

"How'd it go?" Nox asked when he placed the drinks down.

I smiled as he sat. "It went well. I still have to go to

dinner to see my parents because it's been a while, but the date won't be there."

He grunted, and then added, "Good."

What did this man see in me and why would he want to go on a date with me in the first place?

We were complete opposites. He was way bigger and taller than me. Stunningly hot and quieter than I was.

However, I was grateful to Nox for stating it was a date or I wouldn't have been so forward to guess. Spending time with him would help appease my curiosity for this man, especially since I hadn't been able to stop thinking about him.

I blinked over at him. He stared back with a small, soft smile before he took a sip of his drink.

He wasn't an illusion.

I was on a date with Nox Blackwood.

With the man who'd plagued my dirty dreams for months. I never thought I'd get the chance to see him again, yet here I was in a diner about to eat with, quite literally, the man of my dreams.

I only hoped he didn't turn into a nightmare.

Please let this man be the one. Please.

"So, um, can I ask some things about you?" When he tipped his chin up at me, I asked, "What were you doing with Rio in class if you weren't taking it?" After the first time seeing him, I'd looked at my class list and hadn't found anyone new, so I figured he hadn't been in my class to learn.

"My brother is very protective of his m—husband. He asked me to watch over him for the day."

I wanted that type of dedication.

"Oh, wow, that's really sweet."

"Do you enjoy being a professor?"

"Um...." I picked up my drink and took a sip while I thought it over. Clasping the glass, I shrugged. "I used to love it a lot. Even when I was scared to stand in front of everyone and talk. But now it feels like it's missing something. I could just need a change in the subject I'm teaching. Then again, I find it harder these days to get motivated to teach. The students like to laugh at me, which I can't blame them. I can be a klutz. I should be over getting laughed at, but it still plays with my mind a little. Heck, maybe I should just get a different job where I don't have to be around people."

Nox suddenly leaned forward with intense anger in his gaze. "I can make them stop laughing at you."

"H-How?"

He made a clicking sound with his tongue and leaned back, shaking his head. "Never mind how. I would do it, for you."

Throwing myself at this man would be wrong, right?

As a professor, I shouldn't condone the violence he was offering, which I'd read from Nox's tense form and hard gaze, especially against my students, but I still melted from the thought of Nox wanting to look out for me.

"Thanks for offering, I think, but I'll figure something out. Even if I do search for a different job. One I'm more passionate about."

Nox slid a finger around the rim of the glass. "I could see you working in a library."

I cocked my head to the side. "Why's that?" And how did he know that had been a job I considered but brushed it away because of the encouragement from my parents to become one of the youngest professors.

Nox's hand stilled. He glanced up at me. "You like to read, don't you?"

Laughing, I pushed my glasses up. "Are you insinuating I'm a book nerd because of the eyeglasses?" I hoped he took my words in a teasing way, like I'd intended.

His smirk put me at ease. "Maybe," he teased back.

A waitress arrived with our meals and after she placed them on the table, then left, I asked, "Can I ask what you do for a living?"

He tipped his chin up my way. "My brothers and I own many businesses that we oversee from our main building in the city."

Dang, he sounded busy. Nodding, I picked up my burger and bit into it.

"However, we have a strong, loyal team that surrounds us, which frees up our time. I go into the office only a few hours a day."

Swallowing the food down, I then said, "That sounds like a great way to live."

He'd have more free time for other things.

Like me.

God, I was being selfish thinking of myself when it came to Nox and wanting more time with him, but I couldn't seem to help it.

I already wanted to know when I could get another date. Would he even want another date? If yes, *why* would he want one?

If things went well and I didn't mess this up somehow,

I could see a lot of dinners in our future, which could lead into sleepovers.

My cock throbbed in my pants at the thought of naked Nox in bed with me.

First date, first date, first date. I had to keep reminding myself that and slow down. I didn't want to come off as being too easy, even though I wanted to see how his lips felt against mine. Immediately, more thoughts bounced around in my mind. Would he fill me the way I liked? And his scent.... I took a subtle whiff. I needed to know what his cologne was. I wanted to bottle it and keep it forever, maybe have some by my bedside as I was sure I could come untouched from inhaling it.

"We enjoy it." His eyes unfocused for a moment, tearing me away from my wayward thoughts. Staring at his gaze, I saw a colder side that had me shivering. Before I could take a breath, he blinked and the intensity was gone.

Where had his mind gone?

"Are you all right?" I asked softly.

His brows pinched, his jaw ticked, and he looked down at his food, picking up a fry. "My brothers and I have another job." He popped the fry into his mouth and chewed.

"Oh?" I took a sip of my soda as tension tightened my shoulders. I was sure it was a reaction to Nox's stillness.

"You may not like this job, but you need to know before agreeing to go on another date with me."

Heck yes, he wanted another date already.

The tension fled as glee had me mentally fist-pumping the air and whooping with joy.

"I'm sure it can't be that bad." I hoped and prayed.

He glanced around before giving me his full attention. "We accept jobs from the... government. They're not good jobs, Kieran. We... take out people who have done bad things."

A blast of shock had my lips parting.

His jaw ticked again, and he glanced away, but I caught the brief scrunch of worry in his expression.

Closing my mouth, I went to reach across the table for his hand, which he had fisted beside his plate, but I stopped shy of touching him. He peered down at my hand.

"Nox, are you telling me you're an assassin?"

He lifted his head. "In a way, yes."

"Should you be telling me this? Can it get you into trouble?"

"You're worried about me?" Confusion danced in his gaze. "Why are you not worried about yourself?"

"Oh, I never thought about that." I waved it off. "But it doesn't matter."

"Your life does matter. But know I would protect you. I won't let any harm come to you or yours."

My heart turned to mush and melted down to my stomach, which swirled up a storm.

This man was unbelievable. In a good way.

He was like a dream, not only for promising me protection but for also talking about a future date.

But wasn't it too soon?

"I... I don't mean to sound ungrateful that you're placing your trust in me about your profession. I am. But...." Why was I questioning this? He'd been all I could think about, and it was all from just a single glance. Maybe it'd been the same for him too. "You don't think it's too soon to confess your work to me? Or to predict you'll want to see me again when our first date hasn't even ended?"

When his hand brushed over mine and held it loosely, my pulse kicked up.

"It's not too soon. When I first saw you, I had to force myself to walk away, even when I wanted to stay to listen to you. To watch you. I felt there was something in that quick moment. I haven't been able to get you out of my mind."

My ears rang from how fast my organ beat.

"Same," I whispered.

"I already know I'd like to take you on another date, and that one won't be our last either. But I need you to be sure you want this with me, Kieran. After knowing about our work...."

I didn't have to think about it. I already knew.

There was something special about Nox Blackwood. I wouldn't give up my chance at dating this man for anything.

Even with his job killing bad people.

"Yes, Nox. I already know I'd like to go on another date."

The smile he gave me had me soaring.

NOX

How the fuck did I get into this position? Yeah, that was right. I'd stupidly answered Kieran's phone last night when he'd gone to the bathroom. Seeing his mom's name flash up on his screen, I'd assumed she was ringing to try and persuade him into the date she wanted to organize.

Instead, I found out how cunningly clever that woman was.

I'd thought I would have had the control over the conversation, but I hadn't. At all.

"Kieran's phone. This is Nox," I'd answered.

"Nox. You must be the man on a date with my son."

"Yes, ma'am."

"It's been over an hour; things must be going well."

I'd stopped myself from saying it wasn't any of her business and instead grunted.

"Good. You'll come to dinner at our place tomorrow night with Kieran."

My brows had shot high. "I don't think—"

"Six p.m., and don't be late."

"Kieran might not like—"

"Do you want me to invite another man for our son, or are you serious about him?"

"I'll see you then."

"Enjoy the rest of your date, Nox." And she'd hung up, but before she had, I'd caught her squeal of happiness. Then she'd called out to her husband, Drew.

And that was how I called Riker earlier today to watch Kieran from afar—I didn't dare ask Riker to guard my mate in the same room, never knowing what he would say —so I could head home to get ready.

Kieran wanted to pick me up for this date. I didn't like that. I wanted to be in control, but when he'd looked at me with his doe eyes while biting his full bottom lip, I couldn't say no.

Pacing the front entrance, I heard a car hit the driveway, so I went to the window beside the door to peer out. Kieran drove up in his black Jeep. Knowing Riker wouldn't be far behind, I wanted to leave before my brother had the chance to say anything to Kieran. I also wanted to be gone before Deacon and Rio returned from visiting Ruth, our foster mother who took us in after we killed our families. Which sounded bad, but those people had deserved it.

Opening the front door, I stepped out and started down the stairs just as Kieran pulled to a stop.

When I went to grab the handle, I cursed at seeing Riker's bike speeding over the cobblestones. What was worse was Deacon followed close behind.

Groaning, I swiped a hand over my stubble.

Kieran popped out of his side of the car, and I cursed silently again.

He smiled over at me, flushing as he waved and said, "Hi."

I wanted to kiss him.

Last night when I'd dropped him to his house, I'd second-guessed everything so hadn't stolen that first kiss. Seeing him looking adorable as fuck, all I wanted to do was stalk around the car and claim his mouth in a heated kiss.

"Nox?" he called over the car as Deacon pulled to a stop just behind Kieran to block us in.

"Come here," I ordered, keeping an eye on my brothers. They'd better not say anything stupid to upset Kieran or their blood will spill.

Kieran jolted from my demand but walked around his Jeep. With my hand to his waist, I ushered him behind me while I faced Deacon.

My brother stood from his car with a blank expression. Rio scrambled out and went around to Deacon's side, gripping his arm.

"He's bigger than you," Kieran commented with a touch of fear scenting off him.

Riker skipped over. "Hello, good evening, kind sir. Do you remember me? I'm Nox's brother Riker." He pointed to Deacon. "That's our other brother, who can be a bit of a grumpy bear." He leaned in. "Still, he's nothing on your sour puss in front of you. And you know Rio, intimately."

Deacon's bear flashed in his gaze and a growl vibrated from his chest. My own rolled out in warning. Even the tiger lifted his head and joined in with mine.

"Riker," Rio scolded before he curled himself into Deacon's front. "He didn't mean it like that, Deacon. Kieran was my professor."

"Boo," Riker called. "I was hoping they'd throw fists. I wanted to join in."

Deacon cupped the back of Rio's head and pressed his lips to Rio's in a quick kiss. He took his mate's hand and walked over to us. Kieran grabbed the back of my shirt with one hand as he moved up beside me.

"Is there a problem?" he whispered to me.

Christ. My little, accident-prone mate wanted to stand at my side and help me even when he was scared.

Needing to touch him, I curled my arm around his shoulders and drew him in close, kissing his temple.

"It's fine. Deacon can be an ass, but that's it."

Deacon snorted. "You're the biggest ass out of all of us."

"Yeah, and I'm the ray of sunshine in the family," Riker said.

Rio chuckled. "You are, Riker."

Deacon grumbled. He was annoyed, but not-so-secretly ecstatic that Rio and Riker were becoming close.

Deacon's gaze dropped down to Kieran before meeting mine. "Fated?"

"Huh?" Kieran asked.

Rio grinned and Riker cackled.

"Yeah," I replied.

"Sorry?" Kieran said, peering up at me.

"Don't worry about it."

Riker nodded. "It's a family thing. Until you take his cock—"

"Riker," Deacon, Rio, and I yelled.

My mate's cheeks pinked, and he ducked his head. Arousal, confusion, and humor scented around us. All from Kieran.

"We have to go," I told them.

"Where?" Deacon asked.

Kieran made a small groan. "My family conned Nox into dinner tonight."

Rio and Riker laughed their asses off, but at least Deacon held it back with a cough.

"Do you need us to come for support?" Riker offered.

"Fuck no," I stated with a glare.

"Geesh, okay. Good luck, Kieran. Nox, try and talk for once instead of grunting. It'll help with the in-laws."

"Huh?" Kieran muttered, but Riker had already bounced up the stairs to head inside.

I stared down at Kieran as Rio told him not to worry and asked how his old class was going. My chest ached as it filled with adoration for the man who was smiling, laughing, and chatting with my brother's mate. He seemed at ease at my side. I hoped he stayed content being with me even after he learned what I truly was. A man who enjoyed inflicting fear, pain, and death on others. Who also held an animal within.

Worry thickened my throat.

"Nox," Deacon whispered, low enough that the men at our sides wouldn't hear over their talking. "He's good for you."

"I know."

"He'll like you as you are. Rio did me and I never thought it possible."

How the fuck did he read my mind?

Wait, he likely scented the worry from me.

"I hope so."

"Sorry to interrupt," Deacon said. We all looked at him. "Nox won't want to be late to your parents' place and give a bad first impression."

Kieran's gaze swung up to me.

"He's right." I smiled.

"He smiled," Rio whispered to Deacon, but of course it wasn't quiet enough for my hearing.

I mock glared at Rio, but he grinned in return. Looked like he'd gotten used to my walls.

Kieran nodded before he turned back to Deacon and Rio. "It was nice to meet you, Deacon. I hope to see you both another time."

Rio winked. "You will."

"It's an honor to meet you, Kieran."

"Oh, um, thanks?"

Deacon grinned, and asked me, "When can I tell Ruth?"

Fuck.

"Never," I told him. Our foster mother had stayed in town to get to know Rio. If she found out about Kieran, she wouldn't leave and would want to meet him immediately. Probably tell him things I would never want him to know. I loved her like a mother, but she could be too much.

"Ruth?" Kieran asked.

"Their foster mother. She's a sweetheart."

"She's a menace," I clipped.

Kieran snorted. "You'll think differently of her after you've been to my place."

A shot of nerves hit my gut and twisted it.

"Speaking of which, we really should go," I told him.

After another goodbye, Kieran went around and got behind the wheel while I slipped into the passenger seat.

I was going to fuck this up.

Somehow, I'd do something that showed his parents I wasn't worthy of their son.

Christ, I didn't do everyday chatter.

But for Kieran, I would, and I fucking prayed I didn't screw that up.

What would we talk about?

They'd probably ask me about my parents.

I couldn't exactly tell them I killed them for torturing me daily.

"Nox?"

I jolted and glanced over at my mate. He was drowning in concern for me.

"Sorry, I spaced."

"What's wrong?"

"Wrong?"

His glaze flicked down to my hands gripping my thighs.

Fuck.

I had to be honest. He was my mate, and he'd soon

know I didn't do well around others. I liked my own company. I could handle Ruth, my brothers, and Rio. I also wanted Kieran's attention all the time, but anyone outside that, I barely tolerated.

"Did I say something back there that upset you?" He bit his bottom lips.

He never could.

Placing my hand on his thigh, I squeezed gently. "No, Kieran. I was lost in thought because I'm worried about making a bad impression on your parents. I'm not good at communicating. I know I'm gonna say or do something that'll have your parents'—people who are important in your life—dislike me."

"Nox," he whispered, taking one hand off the wheel to cover mine on his leg.

He sniffed and shook his head. "Having you even think that means the world to me." He snorted. "One date and I'm already taken by you. Don't worry about my parents. I'm sure they'll like you, and even if they don't, us dating has nothing to do with them. It's about you and me."

"You and me," I repeated, wanting to hear his words from my mouth because they had my body feeling weightless.

"Yes." He nodded. "You and me. Just relax and be yourself. God knows I'll talk enough for the both of us." His bright smile shone over at me before he put his attention back on the road.

Lifting his hand in mine, I pressed my lips to the back of his palm and felt him shiver.

Christ, I loved his reactions to me.

I adored so much about him already. For him, it was our second date. For me, I'd been stalking and slowly falling for him for months.

If I'd known he'd felt the attraction from that first glance, and I didn't have doubts about myself and Kieran needing better, I would have pursued him earlier. At first, when Rio showed for Deacon, I'd been fearful of the bond between fated mates. But the concept grew on me once I saw how Deacon and Rio were together. Witnessing their connection and how in sync they were calmed some of my concerns. I hadn't approached Kieran as I was certain he deserved someone better, someone more than my messed-up self who hated most people and the animal that lived inside them.

Since yesterday, I couldn't deny Kieran or myself something that would make us both feel whole. What was growing would be something amazing together, and I didn't give a fuck how cheesy that sounded.

"Glad you want to help me out, Kieran."

I loved saying his name.

"Always," he stated, and I could hear the truth in his tone.

So even though I wanted to upchuck about meeting the parents, I swallowed that down. My mate would have my back, and somehow, we'd get through this together.

CHAPTER SIX

KIERAN

A ball of anger remained lodged in my throat from my mom conning Nox into joining us for dinner. The poor guy was too nice for his own good. Especially for answering the phone in the first place, something I found sweet and courageous. While I'd been mortified when he told me about the conversation, Nox reassured me he really did want to come. And that was how we were in the car now on the way there.

Considering that, I was glad he picked up the phone when Mom called, and she talked him into it. I also hadn't wanted to turn up alone. I wanted Nox at my side all the time in the greediest way possible.

I even wished I could live in his dang pocket so I would never be far from him.

A craving to be by his side was a new sensation. While it scared me, it also exhilarated me. My stomach hadn't stopped fluttering since being around him.

Two days, and I already knew those wouldn't be enough. I wanted to see him tomorrow and the next and the next.

On and on.

However, the bitterness of worry slammed into me every time I thought this was all too much, too soon, and that eventually, Nox would get sick of my clinginess.

For now, I had to brush all my worries and my need to the side to make sure tonight went well.

I wanted everyone to get along and like each other.

Pulling to a stop in my parents' drive of their single story, three-bedroom brick home, I turned off the car and looked at Nox. I placed my hand over his again, which was still on my thigh.

My heart was in a constant state of swooning at his touch, by his reassurance.

"Ready?" I asked.

He swallowed and nodded.

This poor man.

Leaning forward quickly, I kissed his cheek. "I'm sorry you got roped into coming, but thank you for doing this with me."

Something twisted in my chest as I climbed out of the car without waiting for a reply. At least I heard his door open, so I guessed he didn't mind my invasion of closeness.

I waited at my side of the vehicle for Nox and then

started for the front door. Until my wrist was taken in a tight grip, and I was tugged back. I stumbled and landed against a very hard, wide, and warm chest.

I stared at my hands on his firm pectorals.

"Kieran?"

"Hmm?" I patted those muscles, barely believing they were under my palms, and I wasn't dreaming. This was real. *I* was touching Nox Blackwood with *my* hands.

"Eyes, Kieran."

I met his gaze and saw heat within them.

Heat for me.

Wow.

"The cheek kiss was sweet, babe, but I need your mouth."

My heart tumbled. "Now?" I whispered.

"Yeah." His head lowered.

"Okay," I muttered against his lips before he took my mouth in a press of skin, once, twice, and then the kiss changed.

As soon as I fisted his shirt, he wrapped his arm around my waist and drew me even closer. He opened his mouth a little, enough for his tongue to sneak out and run against mine. My lips parted against his so I could tangle and tease my tongue with his.

More, please, more.

The kiss was the first I'd ever experienced that left me tingling and needing more.

We broke away to catch our breaths. His gaze burned hotter with want.

I stared up at him in awe. He was here with me. Wanting to lip lock *with me.*

My cock throbbed, already hard from just one kiss. I wanted his hands down my pants and in return, I would give him the same. We'd stroke over each other's cocks until we—

Stop! I had to stop or else I'd be a puddle of desire.

The smirk on his lips had me worried he could read my mind.

He curled me into his chest again and kissed my temple like he couldn't get enough of touching me. Just the thought had my pulse racing.

"Let's go in," he said.

I nodded. Not that I wanted to head inside, but we really did have to.

He led me with his arm around my shoulders to the stairs. My toe snagged one of the steps and I would have fallen if it wasn't for Nox's quick thinking and movement by swinging out his other arm in front of me to hold me still.

"You okay?"

Patting his arm, I bobbed my head. "I'm good. Heck, maybe I need you around all the time to help me from hurting myself."

"I'm thinking that's a good idea."

Holy guacamole, is he for real? No, he can't mean that... but he said it. Nope, I won't read into it.

At the front door, Nox reached out to knock, but I grabbed the handle, twisted, and opened the door.

"They'll expect me to walk in," I told Nox as I stepped through and waved him in.

He hesitated a little but then stiffly walked by me with

his gaze flicking everywhere around the living room. Like he was looking for trouble.

He wouldn't find any.

Smiling, I closed the door and took his hand in mine. A thrill tingled up my spine with how natural it felt taking it.

"They'll be at the back of the house in the kitchen and dining area."

He nodded.

I kept my hand in his as I walked in front of him down the tight hall. Noises came from the end. We passed the bedrooms and bathroom and stopped at the entrance where Mom slid something out of the oven.

"Drew, get that knife away from my roast. We're not carving it yet."

"Babs, they'll be here soon. We gotta have it ready."

"I'll cut you if you touch it. It's got to rest. Go have a beer or something."

Dad snorted but placed the electric knife down and turned to the refrigerator as I pulled Nox into the room more.

"Holy fuck, you're a big boy," Dad yelled.

Mom spun around and her eyes widened.

A blush bloomed over my face. "Dad," I scolded.

Mom shook off her shock first and dropped her oven mitts on the counter before coming our way. When she neared Dad, she smacked him on the back of the head.

"Hello, welcome, Nox." Mom smiled.

"Thanks for inviting me," he replied and glanced down at me.

I grinned up at him and clasped his hand between both of mine.

Dad cleared his throat and stepped up to Mom's side, holding out his hand. Thankfully, it was aimed at Nox's free hand. "Drew Higgins. The wife is Babette."

Nox gripped and shook.

Dad stared down at their hands. "Jesus, do you eat small children for lunch?"

Nox snorted. "Usually it's just dinner."

Dad chuckled, Mom smiled, and I felt Nox relax since his grip loosened.

"Where did you find this one, son?" Dad asked. He went back to the refrigerator and grabbed two beers. When he came back over, he gave one to Nox.

"Where's my drink?"

He waved me off. "In the fridge."

Rolling my eyes, I dropped Nox's hand and went to get my own while Nox opened his bottle and took a sip.

"Kieran didn't say where you met," Mom said.

"College," Nox replied.

"He's not a student," I called, taking out the jug of iced tea.

Dad guffawed. "We know you'd never go for a student."

"But what do you do?" Mom asked.

"How about we sit down at the table before you two start grilling him? Mom, do you want an iced tea?"

"Yes, please, honey."

"Come sit, Nox," Dad said, and they walked over to the table as Dad asked him what sports he was into.

Mom rushed over to me. "Oh, wow, Kieran, he's a handsome man."

Smiling, I nodded. "I know."

"He must work out."

"I'm pretty sure he does."

Her brows raised. "You don't know?"

I passed her the glass. "Mom, this is our second date. By the way, I can't believe you talked him into coming."

"Honey, it didn't take much for him to agree. I only had to mention having someone else here for you that—"

I gasped and then hissed at her, "You said what?"

"Relax. It showed us that he doesn't want you with another man." She smiled and took a sip of her drink while studying me. "I can already see a change in you."

Shaking my head, I glanced over to the table. "He's.... I hope this works out, Mom." If it didn't, I worried what would become of me. Nox was completely different to anyone I'd ever met, let alone dated. He'd been kinder to me and shown me more attention in such a short amount of time.

Mom laid her hand on my upper arm and gave me an affectionate squeeze. "I have a good feeling about him already."

"Thank you. We'd better get over there before Dad says something embarrassing."

"Good idea. The vegetables won't be too far away, so then we can eat."

When we approached the table, I heard Dad say, "I found out he was gay when I caught him drooling over the players instead of taking in the game."

"Dad!" My face flamed. I took the seat next to Nox,

who grinned down at me. "Don't listen to anything he says."

Mom laughed, sitting next to the father I was about to disown. Wait, could I disown my father? Anyway, he wouldn't be a part of my life if he kept up with those types of stories.

"I never announced my sexuality to anyone because I don't give a fuck what people think." Nox winced and glanced at Mom. "Sorry."

She waved him off. "Don't worry about it. Drew curses like it's going out of fashion and he's trying to bring it back in."

Nox chuckled. The sound warmed my chest.

"Are you a professor as well, Nox? Is that why you met at college?"

Nox shook his head. "Not a professor. I'm a bit older than my... Kieran."

"Aww, he said, 'my Kieran,'" Mom cooed.

Once more, my face flamed. "How old are you?" I asked.

Nox turned to me. "Forty-one."

My lips parted in surprise.

"What skin regime do you use?" Mom asked.

Dad coughed. "You know Kieran is only twenty-seven?"

Mom gently slapped Dad's arm. "You can't talk. I'm eight years younger than Drew." She glanced at Nox.

"That's not fourteen years."

"It's fine," I told him with a glare.

Dad's lips twitched. "As long as you're not gonna call him daddy—"

"Oh God, please, shut up," I whined and palmed my face with one hand while I used the other to slide onto Nox's thigh to keep him from running. "I'm not into that."

"You're making Kieran uncomfortable," Nox said, and I peered up at him to see his gaze had hardened.

I squeezed his thigh, so he looked to me. "It's okay. He's like Riker saying the wrong things, but we just put up with it because he's a part of the family."

As he ran his eyes over my face, I smiled softly at him. I was grateful for his concern.

Nox nodded.

"Who's Riker?" Dad asked.

"My brother. He never thinks before he speaks. We… had a hard upbringing. He's actually my foster brother, like Deacon."

That made a lot more sense to me. They looked nothing alike. But hearing that their life before being fostered was difficult turned me cold.

I pushed my shoulder into his in a way that hopefully showed him my support. He took my hand in his on his lap.

Mom said, "Sorry to hear that, Nox. I'm glad you and your brothers found a better life."

"Thank you. I apologize for snapping at you, Drew."

Dad grinned. "All good, son. It shows me you're looking out for our kid."

Nox released a heavy breath and nodded. What sounded like a purr started in his chest, but it quickly cut off. Still, the sound reminded me of the others I heard from him and Deacon back at Nox's. I'd brushed them off as something their family did with each other, but now I second-guessed myself since I was certain that really had been a purr.

"Kieran?" Mom called.

I jolted and looked away from Nox. "Huh?"

"Nox was just telling us about his businesses, and how you met at college because he was guarding his brother-in-law."

Nodding, I pushed back my thoughts of noises and smiled. "That's right. Deacon is very protective of Rio."

"But Nox said that was ages ago," Dad commented. "How'd you two see each other again?"

Dang.

"Oh, well, um... I was mugged," I told them, and quickly rushed out the rest. "Rio, who is Nox's brother's husband, saw it, stopped it, took me back to their place, and Nox took me home after we had dinner together. All that happened last night."

"What?" Dad barked.

Mum gasped and clutched her neck.

"Did you go to the police? How did it happen? Where were you?" Dad fired off.

A timer went off.

Mom stood, then sat back down. "Tell us everything right now, young man. And before the vegetables are ruined."

"I was walking home from college when—"

"Were you reading? You always get lost when reading. Jesus, Kieran." Dad groaned, already thinking I wasn't paying attention. Didn't matter that was what actually happened.

"Maybe," I muttered. "But," I said quickly before Dad could yell at me, "things turned out fine in the end. Rio saw it happen. So when they knocked me out—"

"They knocked you out?" Mom yelled. She stood and came around the table to feel the back of my head.

I gently swatted her hands away. "I'm okay. It doesn't hurt too much. There was no concussion. I checked for all the signs before I went to bed. I think I may have passed out from fright more than them hitting me. Rio chased them off and took me back to their place to watch over me."

Mom sighed, placing her hands on her hips. "That's really nice of him, but why didn't you go to the police?"

"Yeah," Dad called.

"I couldn't remember what they looked like, and neither could Rio. They didn't get my wallet in the end, so there wouldn't be enough information for them to go off."

Dad turned to Nox. "You'll watch out for him?"

"Dad, that isn't a question for a second date."

"I will." Nox replied with such certainty that my heart leaped.

Dad grunted. "Good." He looked up to Mom, who was now hugging me around the neck. "Babs, I'm gonna carve the meat. Those veggies ready?"

Mom pulled back and patted my shoulders. "I'll check them, but yes, you can carve."

Dad clapped. "Hope you boys are hungry." He got up from the table and went into the kitchen area with Mom.

I leaned into Nox, hugging his arm with both of mine. "Thank you."

His lips twitched as he stared down at me. "For what?"

"Being you, and not running from the house screaming because my parents are weird." *And not running from me.*

He dipped down and kissed my nose. "I will never run."

CHAPTER SEVEN

NOX

When Kieran suddenly pulled over to the side of the road on the way home, I panicked and searched for the threat frantically.

"What's wrong? Is someone following us? Did you see something?"

"Sorry. I'm sorry. I-I just wanted to talk."

Fuck.

I swallowed my heart and rubbed a hand over my face. "Everything okay?"

Red coated his cheeks. I hated that I overreacted, but I'd been lost in thought once again in the car. Proud of myself for not screwing up at dinner and actually enjoying his parents' company, I saw good things for our future. But eventually, once we mated, I'd have to ask Kieran what he wanted to do since Kieran's age would slow to match mine. His parents would have questions. Since Kieran was a fated mate, we could inform them of our existence, if he wanted them to know.

It was something to think and talk about later, though.

"I'm fine." He groaned and ducked his head down. "Just feeling silly now."

Reaching out, I touched a finger under his chin, and he lifted his head so I could have his gaze. "Don't worry about anything you want to do or say around me."

"Okay," he breathed.

I nodded, running my thumb over his chin before dropping my hand. "What did you want to talk about?"

"Oh, um, well...." He scraped his top teeth over his bottom lip before blowing out a breath. His cheeks pinked even more. My heart stuttered. "I don't know if this is too forward or too soon, and tell me if it is, please. You see, I was wondering if you would like to come to my place?"

My cock thickened as my blood pumped harder, faster through my system. I thinned my lips to keep the tiger's purr inside. The animal wanted us close to him all the time. The tiger loved Kieran's attention and was annoyed it'd been so long since the creature got pats and rubs from him.

"I knew it was too soon. Ignore everything I've just said." He faced forward and grabbed the wheel.

Before he could put it in Drive, I placed my hand over his, stilling him. His breathing turned uneven.

"I'd very much like to go into your house. For a drink. For a kiss. For a hug or more. Anything you want, Kieran.

We'll take it at your pace. Just know that tomorrow, you'll come to mine for dinner and then a sleepover. Maybe even the next night, and the next, and the next."

Laughter burst out of him, all relief and joy. He wrapped his arms around my neck and buried his face into my chest. I listened to him inhale on a shaky breath as he held me tighter.

I ran my hands up and down his back and pressed my nose into his hair to inhale.

Mate.

Mine.

"Kieran?"

He huffed, pulling back, and I regretted saying anything because now he was on his side of the car.

"Sorry, you, um, overwhelmed me and made me happy, like I've never felt before. I had to hug you."

Laying my hand on his thigh—something I liked to do often as it meant I got to touch him—I ran it up and down a little.

"Hug me anytime you want."

He bit his bottom lip around a smile as he nodded and started to drive.

When we pulled to a stop out the front of his small but cute—much like him—house, I reminded myself that I had to pretend I hadn't been here.

I hadn't been inside already.

I definitely hadn't looked around or watched him sleep or listened to him on a call or singing off-key in the shower.

Christ, I really was a creepy fucker.

I worried for Kieran in our future. I suspected I'd try

to get inside him any chance I could since it was the closest that I could be with him without carrying him everywhere I went. That way I didn't have to go a second without seeing him.

Fuck me.

I was screwed.

At least Kieran, so far, wasn't running for the hills from me. Then again, he didn't know about my stalking yet.

When we got out of the car, I met him at his side to make our way into the two-bedroom, one-bathroom house.

A place Kieran had made homey with his little decorations and furniture that suited him to a T. Did he like our place? Did he think it too much? It *was* too much, but Deacon and I couldn't find it in us to say no to Riker after he'd fallen in love with the mansion.

Kieran's home had an open-plan living, dining, and kitchen at the front. At the back were the bedrooms and bathroom, which included his washing machine and dryer. It was so unlike my home where a person could easily get lost in it.

Kieran gave me a tour and, on the way back out to the living room, I said, "Deacon and I hate our place. It's too big. Riker saw it, fell for it, and he'd been so excited we couldn't say no."

In the living room, Kieran turned to me and reached out to run a hand down my arm. He stopped at my hand and held it.

"Don't feel bad for having a bigger place than mine. I'm happy with this house. It's all I've ever needed because

I'm on my own. You have your brothers to consider, and I think it's really sweet that you and Deacon gave in for Riker."

With his hand in mine, I tugged him into me, knowing he would easily fall, and cupped the back of his neck.

Kieran tipped his head back and pushed his eyeglasses up his nose before resting his hands on my chest. My cock throbbed when I saw the lust in his gaze.

"I'm going to kiss you now," I told him. If he didn't want this, he needed to tell me. I had a feeling, one that put fire in my lower gut, that my mate wanted more from me.

"Okay," he whispered in a needy way that had my dick aching. He swallowed thickly before smiling softly.

I kissed his temple, and he sighed. I kissed his nose, and he grinned. I touched the tip of my tongue to his top lip for a quick lick and taste, and he shivered.

"Nox," he panted.

I traced my tongue over his parted lips and his swept out to play with mine. I came undone and deepened the kiss. His eyeglasses got in the way a little, but not enough to stop us.

His hands dropped to my waist and gripped. I slid mine down his spine to stop just above his pert ass. I'd been admiring his butt since I started my stalking. I wanted to bite it, nip, suck, and lick all over it. I bet it would be as smooth as the skin I was suddenly feeling with my fingers up under his tee.

But then I remembered we needed to breathe, and

that I didn't want my mate passing out. I drew back with a small peck to his nose.

Still panting, Kieran pressed his forehead to my chest. His hands tightened at my waist.

"Nox." His hungry tone sang to me. Had me wanting to give him more.

We couldn't have sex. I didn't have enough strength not to bite him, which would finalize the bond.

Still, I could please him in other ways.

Dipping down, I kissed his neck and felt his shiver. I threaded my fingers through the top of his hair and tugged his head back.

He dropped a dirty moan as I stared into his hooded emerald gaze.

"Need to taste you, Kieran. Want your cock in my mouth. Want your cum down my throat. Will you let me have it?"

He licked over his lips, eyes widening in a shocked and dazed gaze. "I-I would like that."

A purr slipped out, the tiger liking the idea of Kieran's flavor on our tongue.

Kieran's brows pinched together. "What's that—"

"On the couch, Kieran. Undo your pants and pull your cock out. I want it ready and waiting for my mouth."

His lips snapped closed, and as I let him go, he wavered but steadied himself, nodding. I hated that the distraction worked, but I knew what he'd been about to ask.

Those answers would come, just not yet. I wanted to drink my mate down first.

I scraped my top teeth over my bottom lip and fisted my hands as I watched Kieran walk over to the couch. I heard him undo the button and zipper to his jeans before he pushed them down a little, revealing half of his smooth ass cheeks.

Fuck.

A stab of arousal hit me and I groaned low.

He glanced over his shoulder with a flushed face as he smiled shyly. He pushed his frames up his nose, turned, and sat. Before my mate leaned back, he pulled his tee up and off his slim, toned body.

Christ.

He was utter perfection.

My feet ate up the floor, and I stopped just before him. "Spread your legs, baby."

He stared up at me, breathing hard, and slowly parted his legs. I dropped to my knees between them and rested my hands on his thighs.

"You gonna make me work for it, Kieran, or you gonna offer me up your cock?"

His hand shook when it pushed into his jeans and pulled out his erection with a pink, leaking tip.

A punch of desire smashed into my lower gut and my cock throbbed.

I slid a hand up his thigh and as he used a finger to angle his dick my way. I wrapped my hand around his length as he let go, sucking in a sharp breath and moaning out my name.

Christ, yes.

"Watch me, baby," I ordered, and lowered myself over him to lick around his cockhead and through his slit before groaning over the drop of precum I tasted and swallowed down.

"Nox, more, please. *Please*." His fingers corded through my hair, locking and unlocking.

I took him in, sucked him down, and hummed around him.

"Oh yes, Nox."

With my other hand, I tugged his jeans down to cup his balls and gently rolled them around while I bobbed up and down on his silky, wet cock.

With another hum and suck to his length, I lost a hold of his balls as they drew up. My mate was close. I was going to get to gulp his cum down and savor the taste.

Fuck.

My own dick ached, needing a release.

A pure yearning to mark my mate in my own scent had me reaching down to undo my jeans. I pulled my prick out, gripped Kieran's leg as I straddled it and locked it between my thighs to thrust my hardness into his shin.

"God, yes, Nox. Yes!" Kieran cried. He ran his hands over my hair, neck, shoulders, and down under my shirt to my back where they continued their exploration. Like he needed to touch me as much as I did him.

I rolled my hips into his leg faster and faster. The bite of climax hit my spine.

Groaning around Kieran's cock, I sucked him deeper and swallowed.

"Nox," he yelled and moaned through his release that I gulped down. His sweet, salty taste that I wanted to savor on my tongue had me crashing closer to the end.

With a couple of more thrusts, I lost myself and soaked Kieran's jean-clad leg. I should have been appalled at my behavior of humping him like a damn dog, but even as I pulled my mouth off his cock with a wet pop, I drew in my scent covering him and smirked in pride.

I wasn't the only one happy.

The tiger strutted inside me. But at least I hid my joy by laying my head on his lap and circling my arms between him and the couch.

"Stay the night?" Kieran panted as he patted my back.

I nodded and guilt had me saying, "I made a mess of you."

His laughter was light. "I know. I liked it."

I grunted and quickly thinned my lips to stop the purr.

"Good," I told him.

"Nox?" He absently tickled over my back, still under my shirt. I wanted to remove the clothing so he wasn't restricted and could explore anywhere he liked.

"Hmm?"

"I like your tattoos. Do they mean anything?"

"No. When I saw the artist's designs, I wanted them, so I got them. Besides, I enjoy the sting of the needle."

"Really? I hate needles."

I chuckled lazily, feeling the start of sleepiness after an explosive orgasm. "Then maybe it's best you don't get one."

"I agree."

I hugged him tighter to me.

"Maybe we should take this cuddle session to bed?" he suggested.

Swiftly, I stood and picked Kieran up with me. He let

out a gasp but then beamed up at me, curling his arms around my shoulders.

His nose screwed up a little. "Though, a shower could be good." Good idea since we were both covered in my cum.

Chuckling, I kissed his neck and against it, I said, "I'll help wash you."

He shivered. "Yes, please." Kieran rested his forehead to my shoulder as I carried him toward the bathroom. "I have work tomorrow." He let out a groan of irritation.

"Can I borrow your car to drop you off, and then I'll pick you up before you come to my place?"

His head popped up with surprise written in his wide eyes. "You want to do that? I mean, drop me off and pick me up? What about your work? I don't want to disturb—"

I shushed him with a quick kiss.

He didn't know that seeing him to and from work would ease my stress.

"I know you usually walk—"

His brows pinched. "When did I tell you that?"

My gut tightened.

Shit.

He hadn't.

I knew it from watching him.

"Ah, I figured as much since you were walking when Rio helped you."

"Oh, well yes, I do prefer to walk. But having you take me to and from the college would be nice."

"Good." I kissed his nose, relaxing from my slipup. "We'll plan it out more tomorrow morning." I nipped at his neck, and he tilted it to the side to give me more access. I licked up it, enjoying his taste in a low hum. "Let's get clean and to bed."

Where I would hopefully talk him into letting me drink his cum down one more time.

CHAPTER EIGHT

KIERAN

A storm of butterflies fluttered in my stomach as I headed for the college exit where Nox waited for me. It honestly still astounded me that Nox wanted to see me again and so soon. He wanted me at his house for dinner, around his family, and to stay the night.

Me, Kieran Higgins, was wanted by the most handsome man I'd ever laid eyes on.

I couldn't stop smiling and praying that this would last forever.

"Kieran" was called, and I turned to see Professor Portley Jeffers. Port was a thirty-something nice-looking man who taught psychology. I sometimes went out with him, in a group setting, for drinks.

"Hi, Port," I said as he stopped beside me, and I pushed my frames up my nose.

I waved him forward, wanting to get outside quicker. He fell into step as he asked, "We're thinking of drinks this weekend. The same group as usual. Would you consider?" Just as I opened my mouth to decline, his hand shot up for me to hold my thought while he used the other to open the door. "Before you say no, just think about it a little longer. You haven't gone out with us in a long time, Kieran. We haven't even heard about your holiday."

I smiled. "It wasn't anything special."

"Still, you need to get out more."

Sighing, I stopped on the footpath. "The last time I went with all of you, I embarrassed myself when I slipped on the ice and knocked into a group of bikers."

He started laughing. "I know. It was fun."

"For you. I nearly soiled myself thinking they were going to kill me."

He reached out and gripped my shoulder, still chuckling. "I'm sorry, but the look on your— Holy shit," he whispered.

Hands landed on my waist while lips pressed against my neck. I didn't have to guess who it was. My body already recognized his. I closed my eyes and smiled.

"Nox," I breathed.

"Remove your hand." I shivered at Nox's hard and harsh tone.

I glanced up at him to see he was glaring at Port. Swinging my gaze to my colleague, I witnessed his gulp as he slowly dropped his hand. It was as if he didn't want to startle Nox with fast movements, which made me want to laugh, but I pressed a fist to my stomach. Nox was a gentle giant, but from the death look he was still giving Port, maybe he'd been just showing me his sweet side.

Warmth blossomed inside me, knowing he found me special enough to share that side of him.

"Nox, this is Portley Jeffers. He's a professor as well."

Nox grunted.

"Port, this is Nox my... um...." What did I class him as?

"Boyfriend," Nox supplied.

I peered up at him while my heart beat rapidly in my throat.

Nox claimed me in front of Portley.

Wow.

I'd never had that before. No wonder people swooned over public declarations. My insides felt all squishy and I wanted to kiss him.

Nox dipped his head and laid one on me.

I was sure this man could read minds.

The kiss didn't last long like I wanted it to, but Nox was being respectful. More than aware students and other professors were walking around.

"Your boyfriend?" Portley asked, shock evident in his tone.

"Yes." I smiled, straightening my eyeglasses and leaning into Nox's body at my back. "Port was just asking—"

"No. I wasn't asking anything. I have to go. Bye, Kieran." He nodded at Nox. "Sir." He walked away quickly.

Nox turned me in his arms while I laughed lightly over Portley's reaction to Nox. I understood how Nox could come across as intimidating. I had been when in his office that day. That was until I got to be alone with him and he'd come to life more.

Nox's jaw ticked while he watched Portley escape.

Reaching up, I gently tapped his jaw. His attention dropped down to me and he finally grinned.

"Kieran," he said softly before laying another quick kiss against my lips. When he pulled back, he added, "I don't like that man."

Snorting, I shook my head. "He's just a friend. We sometimes go out for drinks with a group of other people."

"You've never dated him?"

"Portley? No."

Nox's jaw clenched. "He wants you."

Laughing, I rolled my eyes. "He doesn't."

"He does. I can tell."

When he went to look the way Portley had gone, I cupped the side of his face to keep him in place. "Even if he does, which I doubt, I wouldn't do anything with him. I'm fully committed to see where this goes with you, Nox."

He grunted, but I could tell he was happy with my declaration when the corner of his lips tipped up and his eyes warmed.

"Let's go grab your bag from home and get to my place."

"Okay," I whispered while my belly swooped.

"YOU'LL TELL me if any of my brothers piss you off?" Nox asked for the third time as we made our way to the door from the garage that led into the house.

Smiling, I nodded and squeezed his hand. "What will you do if I did say they were?"

"I'll gut them."

He said it with such a straight face that I stumbled over nothing. I would have fallen if it wasn't for Nox wrapping his other arm around my waist.

He gently tugged me around to face him, gently pinching my chin so I looked up at him. "I'm going to need to be by your side twenty-four-seven so you don't hurt yourself."

Grinning, I told him, "That's sweet, but I don't want to be a burden. Also, I've lasted this long without killing myself, I'm sure I'll be fine."

He shook his head and went to say something, but then I gasped when I remembered.

"Fluffy! Can I see the tiger, please?"

His expression blanked.

"Nox?"

Had it been rude of me to ask about the tiger? I was excited to spend the night in his domain too.

"Sorry, you probably think I'm here just to see him. I'm not."

"Later, maybe." Worry teased my innards at his curt

answer. His hands dropped away from me, and he picked up my bag again—not that I noticed him dropping it—to turn and stalk the rest of the way to the door. "I've fucked up."

I didn't think he wanted me to hear what he'd said quietly, but I'd been right behind him, ready to reach out and stop him.

Until those words stalled me.

What had I done wrong for him to think he'd messed up? Did he think it was too soon now? Did he want me to go?

Ice settled into my veins.

Pressing a hand to my stomach, I took a step back. "I can go."

He faced me on a spin. "What?"

"I heard what you said. If I've done something and you don't want me here, I... I can go." I bit my bottom lip to stop it from trembling. I glanced away, pushed my frames up as my eyes welled.

No, no, no. I will not cry. That's stupid to even want to. It's fine. Everything is fine. If he doesn't want me, I'll get over it.

I was kidding myself into thinking that. I'd thrown my feelings into the Nox basket. I didn't want to take them out, but there may not be a choice.

I jolted when he dropped my bag.

My head swam when I forgot to breathe for a moment as he charged at me.

When Nox picked me up on his way back to the car, panic clawed inside me, until he sat me on the hood and stepped between my legs that he'd separated.

Nox's warm palm pressed over my chest, and he rested the other on the back of my neck. I drew my gaze up to his heated one and gasped.

A sound rumbled out of him, one that sounded awfully like a purr. I lifted my shaky hand to his chest and felt it move under my palm.

"How do you make that sound?" I asked softly, then added, "*Why* do you make that sound?"

A heavy need punched me in the belly, and I had to rest my ear against his chest. Closing my eyes, I placed my hand at Nox's waist and the sound got deeper, faster.

It could easily lull me to sleep. I wanted to hear it all the time, but what I needed more was to know how and why he made it.

Pulling back, I locked my gaze onto his and reached up to brush my thumb over his bunched brows. When they smoothed out under my touch, I told him, "It's beautiful, but can you tell me how and why?"

The door that led inside the house burst open. "You're here!" Riker yelled.

He skipped in and danced around Nox when my boyfriend went to grab for him. "Out," Nox grumbled.

"No way. You got Kieran to yourself last night. It's my turn to get to know him." Riker shoved his brother. My mouth dropped open when Nox actually stumbled to the side.

Tiny Riker was able to move Nox, who was twice his size.

Riker stepped between my spread legs, turned, and I managed to wrap my arms around his shoulders before he grabbed my legs and raced into the house with me clinging to his back.

There was a crash in the garage behind us, which made Riker laugh like a madman.

"Riker!" Nox snarled loudly.

A carefree chuckle escaped me. I couldn't help finding humor in their brotherly fighting, especially knowing they were assassins too. Riker was easy to take to with his carefree attitude and how he teased Nox.

Riker probably read his brother's tension from my questions and acted to fix it.

It was sweet.

Still, I couldn't stay at the side of the troublemaker for too long.

"Riker," I said. "Put me down before—"

"What the fuck are you doing?"

I looked down the end of the hall to see Deacon standing with his arms crossed, scowling at his brother.

Riker stopped but didn't let me down. "Having fun. It's been soooo boring lately."

"Place Nox's... guy on his feet slowly and gently, Riker."

I heard heavy footsteps from behind and knew it was my boyfriend bearing down on us. However, I was also still wondering why Deacon hesitated over what to call me. Unless he didn't remember my name.

Riker groaned in annoyance. "But—"

"Now." Deacon's low growl, coupled with something flashing in his eyes, had the hairs on the back of my neck rising.

I pushed at Riker's shoulders with an urgent need to do as Deacon said, fearing that Riker's life was on the line.

"He's letting me down," I called. Riker slowly placed me on my feet. "See, no harm," I told him. But then I took a step away, tripped on nothing, and landed on my ass.

A roar swept down the hallway.

I screamed and scrambled to the side, pressing my back to the wall as I peered down to where Nox stood breathing heavily.

"Nox, don't," Deacon warned.

Riker's hand shot up in front of him. "I didn't push him," he said. He could have convinced him if he wasn't smiling.

"I-I fell," I told Nox, but his gaze was trained on Riker.

More footsteps slapped to the wooden floor and Rio appeared behind Deacon. However, his husband moved in front of him to block him as Deacon warily eyed Nox.

"Nox, calm down," Deacon ordered. I went to stand up, but Deacon said, "Don't move, Kieran."

I stilled.

"Come on, brother. I was just playing." Riker laughed.

I was sure it was the laugh that sent Nox over the edge.

A gun appeared in his hand, and he fired off a shot. I yelped, covering my ears, and watched as Riker twitched his shoulder back before blood spread over his blue tee.

"Nox!" I yelled as I got to my feet and stood in front of Riker. "Are you okay? What do I do?" I fluttered my hands around him, not sure if I should touch him. "We should call an ambulance. Wait, they'll take too long.

Maybe we can drive you?" I nodded to myself. "*I* can drive you. Let's go to the car. Oh God, that's a lot of blood."

Riker reached out, using his shoulder without a dang bullet in it, to pat me on the head. "It's okay," he told me with a grin.

Why wasn't he worried?

Why would Nox shoot him?

I spun on Nox, who had moved down the hall while I fussed over a bleeding Riker, and he now stood hovering behind me. "Why did you shoot your bother?" I smacked him in the stomach.

"He's fine," he grumbled with his upper lip rising when his gaze locked on Riker. I had a feeling he wanted to do it again. At least he didn't hold the gun any longer. But that didn't mean he couldn't make it appear again.

Where had he kept it?

No, that didn't matter.

I turned back to Riker. "We need to get you looked at." I placed my hand to his back, ready to help him toward the garage when Rio moved out from behind Deacon.

"Kieran, he doesn't need to see anyone."

"What? Why? That's ridiculous." I pushed my frames up and scowled at them all.

Honestly, their lack of action concerned me. Why weren't they rushing out of the house and throwing Riker in the car themselves? None of them were breathing heavily like I was in panic. They didn't look sick to the stomach like I felt.

As I took them in more, I noticed all of them seemed

relaxed. Even Nox had settled at the sight of Riker's blood on his shoulder.

"Does this"—I waved around to them all—"reaction have anything to do with your assassination jobs?"

Rio laughed but covered his mouth with his hand and switched to a cough when Nox growled.

He *growled*.

A growl that sounded real.

As if there was an animal inside him.

Which was stupid and crazy.

But... when I put it with those other sounds I'd pushed aside.

I pressed a hand to my erratic heart and prayed I didn't pass out. I wanted answers, dammit.

"You told him we're assassins?" Deacon asked.

Wait... Deacon had also growled when he'd thought Rio and I had something at college.

I flicked my gaze from one man to another, over and over while they bantered and talked. Words I didn't take in. Words that sounded muffled over my own breathing.

Only what I was thinking couldn't be real.

It was crazy.

"Where's Fluffy?" I asked in a whisper, and all voices stopped before their attention swept to me. I swallowed and stepped away, my back hitting the wall. "I want to see Fluffy."

"Who the fuck is Fluffy?" Deacon demanded.

"What is going on down here that none of you heard me enter the damn house?" A woman in her early forties, maybe, stood with her hands on her jean-clad hips down the far end of the hall.

Crapity crap.

She'd see Riker bleeding.

She could call the police.

I wanted to help Riker, get him to the hospital, but I didn't want Nox going to jail.

I'd lose him.

Which was why I acted before I thought.

Reaching out, I gripped the back of Riker's tee and somehow managed to pull him back where I shoved him at Nox. "Hide him or you're going to jail," I ordered quickly, softly before I moved in front of them and held my arms out. "Hi. Hi. Hi. Can I help you? Sorry, we were just having a meeting. Was one of the brothers supposed to come see you? They're just finishing up the-the family thing. I can take you to a room to wait."

My heart took the slippery slide down to my stomach.

Dammit again, I didn't know my way around the house. For all I knew, I could walk this woman into a bathroom.

Her arms dropped from her waist, and I glanced up to see her mouth gaping a little.

However, I couldn't read her anymore because I was suddenly spun around and Nox planted his mouth on mine in a searing, mind-blanking, world-tilting kiss.

For a moment, I forgot the situation and who I was.

Until I remembered.

I pushed at his chest, and he drew back with a frustrated noise even though I started to chase his lips with my own. I blinked and reminded myself of where I was, who I was around, and what had happened.

"What are you doing?" I snapped.

He cupped my cheeks, acting like we were alone and Riker wasn't bleeding. "I shot my brother and you're willing to hide it from people?"

My face flamed. "All for selfish reasons," I told him honestly while my pulse thundered.

"What reasons?"

Closing my eyes, I shook my head within his hold.

"Kieran, please. What reasons?"

Opening my eyes, I thinned my lips for a moment and then whispered the fear that had me feeling cold. "You really won't want me to tell you."

"I doubt that."

Drawing in a breath, I whooshed the words out on my exhale, "I'm willing to lie and hide Riker because I already can't imagine my days without you in them." I took a breath and blurted, "I know it's too soon and it probably sounds crazy, but you're the only man who's accepted me and my faults and came back wanting more. I'm not saying I'm addicted to you because you've shown me attention like no one else." I shook my head and touched my chest. "I feel in here like I've known you a lot longer than a few days. Like we're connected on a deeper, new, and exciting level." I snapped my lips closed, worried I'd said too much, but I couldn't help adding one last bit. "I understand if you don't want to see me again and it all sounds—" I let out a *meep* when Nox wrapped an arm around my back and drew me tightly against him as he silenced me with a kiss.

There wasn't a chance I could stop from smiling around the kiss since his actions were a sure sign that he didn't mind my confession at all.

CHAPTER NINE

NOX

𝒜rousal and love broke open inside me and leaked into my pores. I had to have his mouth since it was wrong to take his body in that moment. *Not yet anyway*. The kiss didn't last near long enough. But I allowed Kieran to push me back enough to pant out his breaths and caught him thinning his lips while he straightened his sexy frames as he remembered we had an audience.

"You guys are stinking up the hallway. You two just need to have sex already," Riker said.

Kieran's face flamed and he gripped the front of my tee.

While I locked one arm around Kieran's waist, I used the other to reach back for my brother, but he danced out of the way with a laugh.

"Riker, leave your brother alone," Ruth scolded.

Kieran tensed. He didn't know who she was.

"Mom," Riker whined.

Kieran's head popped up and his brows were high.

His arms dropped from around me and faced Ruth as Riker skipped down the hall and hugged her. All Kieran's questions and thoughts about the noises we made were pushed back as he stared at Ruth, no doubt wondering about Riker calling her, a woman who looked our age, Mom.

Ruth cupped the back of his head. "Sweetheart, be a good fox and go get cleaned up."

Riker sighed, rolled his eyes, then nodded and raced off.

I glued my gaze back on Kieran. His nose scrunched up in thought. At any other time, it was adorable, but I knew that action was over the reminder of an animal when Ruth called Riker a fox.

Before Ruth arrived, I was sure my mate was on the right track by asking about goddamn Fluffy.

Would he recall it all now?

Kieran's lips parted, but then he gasped and coughed. I patted his back gently. He shook his head.

"Her... you... Fluffy... animals," he got out between coughs.

Shit.

He held up a hand and used his other one to smack his chest. I didn't like him hurting himself, so I removed his and replaced it with mine to rub over his chest as well as his back still.

"How about we go into the kitchen so I can finish preparing dinner?" Rio asked.

Kieran finally drew in a deeper breath.

"We'll meet you there," I told them. I got a thumbs-up from Rio, a sympathetic smile from Deacon, and Ruth beamed at me before they all left.

Ignoring the tightness in my chest, I asked, "You okay?"

Please be okay.

I didn't know what I would do if Kieran rejected me because of the tiger.

It huffed inside me. He was already sure Kieran loved him.

Hell, maybe I was on my own in winning Kieran over in accepting everything.

"I-I... I'm confused, and shouldn't I be worried that Riker was shot, by you, but no one is taking him to get checked over?"

"You don't need to worry about Riker. He'll be fine soon."

His grip on my tee tightened even more. "How?"

I didn't know if it would be best to inform him on my own or take him into the kitchen where everyone waited.

Only, Kieran was my mate.

I had to do this.

No, I *wanted* to do this.

And all I could think of was to show him the tiger.

Fucking Fluffy.

The animal perked up, ready to scent mark our mate.

"Come with me." I took his hand and led him to the end of the hall. There I went left to where my offices were.

I glanced back to see Kieran pushing his eyeglasses up as he watched my ass move under my jeans.

Smirking, I faced forward.

Things would be fine.

He'd already confessed he couldn't imagine his days without me. Plus, the goddamn tiger was right. Kieran had been in love with his cuddly form.

Stepping into the room, I shut the door after him and started to strip.

His green gaze widened, and his cheeks pinked. "Ah, I don't think now is the right time to have sex."

"The sex will come, but not now."

"Why?" His blush spread down his neck. "No, I didn't mean to ask that. I know why not now because of your family being in the other room. Is that really your mom? I know you said you were fostered, but she'd have to have been, what? Twelve? Unless she's had Botox or work done." He gulped. "You're really getting naked. Taking everything off. Good God, I shouldn't be thinking about your body and all the things I'd like to do to it."

Chuckling, I shrugged. "I don't mind." I pulled the last sock off and stood before him. His hungry gaze ran over me.

"You asked about Fluffy," I said while my heart pounded so hard in my chest that I was surprised my ribs didn't rattle.

"Yes," he whispered.

I nodded and allowed the animal out.

The shift took moments and in them, Kieran yipped, stumbled back, landed on his ass *again*, and pressed a fist to his mouth.

He gasped and scrambled to his knees while the tiger purred loudly, dipping down to his belly.

We could smell his shock, his awe, his fear, anger, and even amusement, but confusion and some excitement settled there as well.

"Oh my God, oh my God, oh my God." His hand shook as he slowly reached out, but he brought it back in quickly.

Crawling forward, the tiger licked at Kieran's arm.

A smile started to form until his brows bunched together in thought.

Confusion and awe were winning.

Up on his front legs, the tiger pressed his cold, wet nose into Kieran's neck, drawing out a startled laugh. The tiger huffed against his skin and then rubbed his head into Kieran's body. His chest, back, arms, legs, and face were now covered in our scent and finally, Kieran's tension melted away.

Our mate curled his arms around the tiger's neck and hugged him close while pressing his face into the fur.

"*Shifters* are real. Shifters *are* real. They're *real*," he mumbled. "I have one in my arms and *he's* my boyfriend." He let out a little crazed laugh, like he couldn't wrap his head around the idea, but then the proof was right in front of him. His heart thundered, but at least the smell of anxiety and fear had vanished. He pulled back and held my face between his palms. "You're a tiger. A shifter. This is overwhelmingly cool, but... I don't know. Not that I don't know about you. I-I'm still... I'm certain about Nox. Well, you. Wait, can you even understand me like this?"

Kieran gasped and moved back as he watched my

limbs, head, torso twist, break, and reshape into my human body. I sat on my ass and quickly drew Kieran between my legs to hug him tightly to me.

"I can," I said softly.

"Nox," he breathed, placing his arms over mine, which I had wrapped around his waist. In shock, he shook in my hold.

"I know it's a lot to take in. You're doing so well for me, baby."

He settled into me more.

"Shifters are real, Kieran. My brothers and I are just some of many."

"Are they tigers as well? No, wait, I remember that woman calling Riker a fox. He shifts into a fox?"

"Correct. And that woman is our foster mother, Ruth. She's a wolf shifter. Deacon is a bear."

"Bear!" he yelled. "Oh my God, no wonder he's huge. What about Rio?"

"Human. Like you."

Unease scented off him. "What are you leaving out? I felt you tense."

Hell.

"It's nothing bad. At least, I don't think you'll consider it bad."

He adjusted himself to sit to the side so he could stare up at me. "Tell me, please."

I nodded, cupping the side of his neck. I brushed a thumb over his fast pulse. "Rio is Deacon's fated mate."

His brows pinched in the middle. "What does that mean?"

"To shifters, a fated mate is a rare and precious gift of

someone who is perfectly matched to us. Who we'll love and cherish for the rest of our years."

"Nox." He licked his lips and then blew out a breath. "Am I yours?"

"Yes. It's why you feel strongly for me and I do you. However, don't think this connection that's building is based on the magic of Fate alone. The attraction for each other has to be there to begin with before the link can take. I knew as soon as I scented you that you were mine. I'll do anything to make you happy, feel cherished, and be protected. At the start, I even thought I had to keep you safe from me and my world. Which was why I stayed away for those months after seeing you."

"What changed?"

"Riker pointed out that I didn't give you a choice."

"You took me home that night to see if I wanted more with you."

Grunting, I glanced away before looking back down to him. "Yes. To see if you could want me, but to also protect you from yourself."

He snorted through a laugh. "What?"

"That's not important right now. I do have to be honest to you about something, Kieran. Before you jump in the deep end with me, you need to know more."

Tension locked his body. "Okay."

"I didn't exactly stay away from you in those months."

"What do you mean?"

Sighing, I dropped my head back and stared at the ceiling while silently praying.

"Nox?"

I dipped down and kissed his forehead. "You might

not like the next part, but I won't keep it from you. I couldn't stop what I did even when I tried. You were locked in my mind and I.... Fuck." I drew in an unsteady breath. "Pretty much, I stalked you. It was me, not Rio, who assisted with those—" My jaw clenched. "—*muggers*. I made sure you got to work and home safely. I followed you to the shops, your appointments, and any time you went out or home... or while you were sleeping because I worried you would choke in your sleep. Knowing your luck, it was a possibility, Kieran. I didn't know an uncoordinated person existed before, until I saw you. The stress of leaving you alone and at risk of you killing yourself was too much for me. I had to keep you safe. I had to protect you. Then, when you asked Rio about me, I had to talk to you. Riker may have given me the push I needed, but I was already obsessed with you."

He was stiff in my arms.

Worry gnawed and scratched under my skin.

"Also, my brothers and I aren't assassins. We kill who we're ordered to by our shifter council. We're murderers. I killed those muggers who touched you, harmed you. They weren't going to stop at taking your wallet. They wanted to rape and kill you. I know this because I got it out of them before I took their lives. I'm not saying it's justified; it's not. I could have called the police, but I didn't. In my eyes, they touched what was mine to protect. They deserved nothing but death."

Jesus Christ. My ears rang and my head swam. Had I just fucked it all up?

I had.

I'd fucked up.

My mate was such a soft soul, he wouldn't be able to handle what I'd confessed. I'd said too much and now he would leave. It wouldn't surprise me that if I dropped my arms from around him, he'd run from the room screaming.

The tiger purred, trying to calm me.

I couldn't be calm.

"I'm sorry," I said softly into his hair, taking in his scent, maybe for the last time.

CHAPTER TEN

KIERAN

My stomach was on its own choppy boat ride with how unsteady it sailed over the waves. I knew from reading countless paranormal novels that Nox would be able to scent my anxiety, but I couldn't stop.

What was I supposed to say? What was I supposed to do? I didn't know since I was still trying to process everything in my head.

Nox said they weren't assassins. But didn't assassins murder people that they were ordered to?

Wouldn't that mean that Nox and his brothers were hired assassins for their council?

The only difference—and I was going off what Nox said about the muggers—was that they didn't only stick to jobs the council ordered them to do. They went ahead and ended anyone who crossed them.

But, only bad people, right?

And Nox had done it for me to keep me safe, and that was only after he found out what they were going to do to me. Maybe I hadn't been their first either. There could have been more.

Why was I defending a killer?

I couldn't forget he'd been my stalker as well.

He'd been following me. *Because he worries so he has to keep watch over me. Protect me.* But he broke into my home.

The confusion of it all had my temples throbbing.

The fated mate business was something else I had to think about.

Even when everything in me screamed to accept anything Nox said, I couldn't. I had to at least give myself some time to let everything sink in.

Yet I couldn't bring myself to walk away. I didn't want to hurt him, and if I stayed longer, maybe it would help me process everything.

My decision would depend on if I saw a life with Nox as he was, since I never wanted to change him.

"You, um, like your job?"

He winced. "It's more a necessity. My brothers' animals call for violence to calm them. The tiger inside me is different, and I'm the one who finds it impossible to sedate the hunger for blood. Our packs... they fucking messed us all up, and this is my coping mechanism. Without it, I fear what I'd become if I didn't have some type of structure over how I hunted."

The ache in my chest was back. The same pain that squeezed my heart when Nox spoke of his past. He hadn't said much, but I read between the lines. Besides, what he'd gone through was enough to bring this need for blood out.

Rubbing my lips together, I pushed my specs up and asked softly, "Do you mind if, um, I slept on the things I've learned, and we talk about everything tomorrow?"

This was our lives we were dealing with. It wasn't a simple, quick answer. I'd just found out about shifters, fated mates, Nox's jobs and non-jobs, and I needed a little more time to ponder.

"Take all the time you need. I'll drive you home."

I let out a gasp when Nox easily stood with me in his arms and placed me on my feet.

My face flamed when I looked down at his body, only remembering now he was naked.

"Wait." I blinked and shook my head. I drew my gaze up to his and saw the humor in them. "I don't want to go home. Is it silly of me to want to stay for dinner and overnight, but, ah, maybe in another room?"

Was I blabbering? Did I make sense? I wasn't even sure if I understood my reasoning myself.

"I would like that, Kieran."

Some of the tension loosened my shoulders. "Okay." I wanted to hug him for understanding. For giving me this time, even if I didn't need it in the end. Instead, I wrapped my hand around his wrist. "Thank you."

His fingers glided across the back of my hair. "Anything." With a quick kiss to my forehead, he moved to the door. "I'll grab some clothes in the next room and take you to dinner." He stopped with the door open. He didn't seem fazed he was naked and that anyone could see him. Then again, maybe it was a shifter thing.

Though, if I had his perfectly shaped bottom, I would show it to the world.

"Kieran," he called with a light tone.

I dragged my eyes up. His lips twitched but thinned out. "Please don't fear my family. No one will hurt you."

"I know," I said quickly and truthfully. After all, he did say that fated mates were rare and cherished, which told me that most shifters would treat them with care. But I also trusted Deacon and Riker already since they were Nox's brothers. It was easy to read they would do everything in their power to help him.

No matter how much they teased him.

"But...," I added. "Can we not shoot anyone at dinner?"

His chuckle made my stomach swoosh. "I won't take a gun."

"Thank you." I smiled.

Goodness gracious, I was thanking someone for not taking a gun to the table.

How things had changed. But would it be for the better?

I'd figure it out soon enough, but I already leaned toward yes.

I met Nox in the hallway a few moments later. He was dressed in a black tee with gray tracksuit pants.

Had he done that on purpose?

They certainly looked good on him.

Actually, everything suited his body. I was sure he could even make a garbage bag look good.

Clearing my throat, I said, "Let's eat."

"Are you talking to my dick or me?"

Warmth filled my face, and I flicked my gaze up. "Let's go." I marched down the hallway and nearly tripped but managed to stay on my feet so kept going.

I didn't know if I headed in the right direction, but Nox said nothing, so I continued to lead the way.

How could I be shy and awkward after what we did last night?

It was probably because one moment I was asking for time and the next I was drooling over the outline of his half-hard penis, which I wanted to drop to my knees for.

Mentally, I screamed over the mixed signals I sent the poor shifter.

Shifter.

They're alive and in the real world.

Holy heck.

"Left," Nox called, and I turned at the end of the hallway.

I heard Riker first, "Do you think they did it?" I heard a large intake of breath before I rounded the corner. "I guess not." Riker sat at the eight-seater table in the kitchen area with Deacon and Ruth. Rio was basting some meat over by the oven, which smelled amazing.

Ruth suddenly stood. I stopped when I realized she was coming for me with a bright smile. "It's so lovely to meet you, Kieran." She took me into a tight hug. One I returned with some pats to her back.

This was Nox's foster mother. Yet, she appeared to be

around Nox's age. The shock from it had me gaping at her like a fool when she stepped back.

"It's good to meet you too," I said.

I felt Nox's warmth at my back. "Kieran knows everything."

Riker bounced on his seat. "Then why aren't you two completing the bond by fu—"

"Riker!" was yelled by everyone but me.

More heat hit my face. I turned slowly to Nox. "That's how the bond connects us as a fated mate pair?"

"That and a bite," Riker called.

"Riker," Ruth and Deacon snapped.

"You have to bite me while…. Oh my God." I turned to Ruth. "Sorry for speaking of this around you. I just never thought to ask how it was done."

She rubbed at my arm. "It's all right. Ask anything you like. There's no judgement in this house. Not all shifters are blessed with the gift of a fated. I don't have one, but I found someone I wanted to spend the rest of our days with, and we bonded. It's the same process as with a fated, but we don't have the ability to feel our mate's inside here." She touched her hand over her heart. "The connection with your fated is something special. Though, I can understand your hesitation. Rio informed me you've only known my son for a few days, and you only heard about shifters today. I'm sure it was all hard to comprehend, especially about their work. I'm sure Nox has told you to take all the time you need. There's no rush for such a big decision since this will change your life."

A storm of emotions brewed inside me. "How will it change my life?"

Ruth glanced to Nox. I did, too, and saw him nod to her. I startled when my hand was taken by Ruth, who led me over to the table.

We sat down with Ruth on one side and Nox on the other. Deacon was at the head of the table and Riker opposite me.

I felt crowded. Overwhelmed.

"No offense, but can you give Kieran and me a moment alone?" Rio called. "Since I'm the only human fated to a shifter, I think it would be good for just the two of us to talk."

"He's right," Nox stated and stood. He took a step away but was back at my side again, crouching. "Are you comfortable with Rio talking to you?"

A swarm of butterflies took flight in my stomach.

How could he be perfect, but a killer, and a stalker at the same time?

It's because he cares.

I just needed more answers and knew the person who could give me an inside view of it all.

I nodded. "I would like to talk to Rio."

"Out," he ordered as he stood again, resting a hand on my shoulder. "Everyone but Rio and Kieran out."

"I want to stay," Riker piped up.

Nox's chest vibrated with a growl. But it was Deacon who grabbed the back of Riker's tee and lifted him from his seat to carry him out of the room.

"Boo," Riker called.

Quickly, I turned to Ruth. "I'm sorry. You can stay."

She gave me a soft smile. "Rio is the best person to

speak to. We'll be back shortly." She hugged me again before leaving.

Rio grinned when I turned to him. "Come up here while I place the finishing touches to the food."

I went to the counter and pulled out a chair there, sitting. "So, what's it like being fated to a shifter?" I pushed my frames up and tapped my foot to the footrest of the swivel seat.

Rio glanced off toward to the door with a sweet, melty look on his face.

When he met my stare again, he grinned. "Amazing."

My foot stilled. "Really? Did Deacon stalk you and kill people for you as well?"

"Well, in a way, yes." He shrugged. "We met through my criminal, cartel father. Deacon and his brothers were in his place of business to try and get him to stop dealing drugs in their area. He said no of course, but Deacon had already scented me as his. He left without any hiccups and decided to find me to see where my loyalties lay." He grabbed a knife and started chopping some garnishing. "My father was a bad man, Kieran."

"Was?" I asked. I never would have presumed that Rio's father ran a cartel. At college and while I had been teaching him, Rio had always seemed content, not troubled. However, maybe I'd been shortsighted in life. Sheltered in a way where I never took in more than what surrounded me. Disappointment sat heavily in my stomach.

Rio gave me a tight-lipped smile. "Yes, he *was*. They ended his life because no matter what they offered, they knew it would never be enough. However, Deacon also did it to keep me safe. Without his intervention, my life would've always been on the line. You have to understand that in their eyes, a fated mate is the most treasured gift a shifter can receive. They'll do anything in their power to keep us safe. Which is why Nox was guarding me that day. I don't leave the house without someone with me if it can't be Deacon himself. It's more to satisfy their worries than not trusting us when we're out." He waved a knife around. "Precious gift, remember. What you also need to know is that they love us like no one else has before."

There went those butterflies taking off again.

"How long did it take you to make up your mind about Deacon?"

"When he claimed me?"

"Yes."

"Two days or was it one? I think two. And I've never regretted my choice. I doubt I will. No one has made me happier. I used to live in fear and that vanished when Deacon entered my life. I've lost count of the times he's made me smile, laugh, or feel giddy with happiness. I never had anyone close to me, and I knew that after even a few hours with Deacon, I couldn't think of my life without him. It actually scared me to picture it."

Nodding, I gripped the edge of the counter. It was like Rio read my mind. I couldn't see my days without having Nox in them.

But.... "What about their jobs or when they end someone that they're not ordered to?"

Rio rested the knife down. "Kieran, half of their souls belong to an animal. Add in the struggles they had in their younger years, which almost sent them feral. If it wasn't for Ruth taking them in, teaching them control, and showing them ways to heal and deal with their killer instincts, we wouldn't have met them. Their council would've put them down for being too far gone to exist around others. Their job helps them, and I know what nightmarish people they end. With and without orders. What those people—shifters, humans, and others—have done. Sounds cliché, but still I'll say it. They're making the world a better place, and it helps them in return. But believe me when I tell you, they would never hurt anyone without just cause."

Deep down, I knew that already. Nox had told me how he questioned my muggers and only saw ill intent from them. Like I'd thought already, I probably wasn't their first victim, which was sickening.

"I know," I told Rio quietly.

"I'm sure you do. I think the understanding comes with being a fated mate. I also believe that they're not the only lucky ones being in a fated pair. We are too. Deacon...." He sighed contentedly. "He might annoy me sometimes, but he makes me happy. I'm loving life again, and it's damn hot when it comes to bedroom activities." Rio chuckled when my face flamed. "I wasn't experienced before, but I'm loving learning, and the orgasms—"

"Oh my God, please don't." I fanned my face and ducked my head. I didn't mind talking about sex. I just wasn't used to sharing things with close friends since I hadn't any. I mostly had acquaintances. Though the people around Rio's age didn't seem to be shy about talking freely about everything.

Rio laughed loudly. "Sorry." When his laughter

waned, he added, "Seriously though, our group is like having a newfound family. It can be chaotic, especially with Riker around. It can be hard and strange, but in the end, it's all worth taking that jump."

"What about, um... Ruth looks young."

He hummed under his breath and went to turn off the oven. "Shifters age very slowly. She's actually one hundred and fifty-two."

"What?" I spluttered.

He nodded and grinned. "It's the same for fated mates. Our aging will slow and match our mates' eventually."

My heart fluttered. "Okay, um, wow, but what about my parents? They'll notice."

"I asked Deacon about this, about if another fated mate was human and had a good family. He told me they'd get a choice to tell their family, but only if they believe that their family can keep the shifters' existence a secret."

Would my parents?

That was stupid to question. I knew they would because they had only ever wanted me to be happy.

"They'd keep aging, though. I-I would have to watch them die while I stay young for a longer time."

Rio smiled sadly. "Don't we all die in the end anyway? Some before others. Well, unless you're a vampire or fae. But that has nothing to do with us. We're not all invincible, Kieran. I could die tomorrow if I got my head cut of—" A loud, long, and scary snarl sounded from another room. "Sorry, my mate," Rio called. "Another thing to remember, shifters have good hearing.

Don't snark about them under your breath. I've been spanked many—"

"Rio!" Warmth slapped me in the face.

Rio snickered while a wild cackle started from under the table. After sharing a look with Rio, who rolled his eyes, I got off my seat and went to squat beside the table. Riker sat in a crouch, grinning.

"You get shy and blush a lot more than Rio. This is gonna be fun." He scrambled out and popped up to stand as I did. "I got bored and hungry, and you guys were taking *forever*." He reached up and patted my head. "The moral of the story is that we kill, but we're loveable, and you'll be happier with us in your life." He walked over to the counter and jumped up to sit on it, swinging his legs. "And if you want, we can ask the council to gift them a fae amulet so they can age slowly too."

"Wait, that's an option?" I asked, dumbfounded.

"I didn't even know that," Rio said. "Tell us more."

"The council doesn't allow this option for everyone because the magic inside these amulets is just as rare as fated pairs, and they cost a small fortune," Deacon explained as he, Ruth, and Nox entered.

My belly swooped as my heart stuttered as Nox moved closer.

He stopped at my side and rested a hand to my lower back while Ruth said, "It's a choice you can give your parents, and if they want it, then we'll take it to the council. No matter the expense. Since you're in a fated pair, there's a higher chance they'll agree. They want all fated mates to be content in their lives."

More information for me to think about.

I worried my head would explode with too much more.

"Since the bite for us mates gave us the ability to age slowly, can't biting Kieran's parents do the same?" Rio asked, absently rubbing at his neck where Deacon must have bitten him for the claiming.

"The bite can only work on a fated partner," Ruth said. "Even when Grey and I claimed each other without being fated, our bites didn't have the magic in it to connect us like it already has for Rio and Deacon. My bite was a mating claim to accept him as mine, and vice versa. We didn't want other shifters sniffing around each other thinking we're up for attention."

All this biting talk had my cheeks flaming. It reminded me that Nox would have to mark me for this magic to connect us.

Riker snorted in mirth at seeing my hot face. Nox growled, until I leaned into him.

"I need to keep you around more often," Riker commented. "Maybe he won't be such a sour puss with you there."

I tapped my shoe-covered toes into his foot. "Leave your brother alone."

Riker grinned at Nox. "See, even though he hasn't accepted you, he's still protecting you. You're in with a chance, Nox. Not that I see a worthy mate in you. I'd be better for him—Ouch, that hurt." Riker pouted and then laughed while pulling the knife out of his thigh.

I swiveled to Nox and crossed my arms over my chest.

Nox shrugged. "What? I didn't shoot him."

Sighing, I adjusted my glasses. "No harming anyone in

the family."

Nox sputtered, "He deserves it."

I glanced to Riker, who was grinning proudly.

Then I looked to Ruth for some assistance.

Her brow quirked up. "I've often thought about stabbing my sons."

"Oh my God," I muttered.

"Riker, show him your leg," Rio said. "Shifters can't handle anyone saying shit about their mates. Riker plays on this to stir trouble. I used to get upset on Riker's behalf, but he really does bring it on himself."

I presumed Riker would roll up his tracksuit pants, but he used the hole Nox had stabbed into them and stuck his fingers in to rip them apart. He wiped away the blood with his palm and I gasped.

Apart from a red line, there was no hole. It had completely healed.

"How?" I breathed, gripping Riker's legs to take a closer look.

"He's touching me," Riker sang.

"Shut the fuck up," Nox snarled.

Ignoring them, I grabbed the roll of paper towel off the counter, tore some off, and wiped more blood away. Even the red mark was fading.

"Shifters heal quickly from small wounds. If we shift, we heal faster," Ruth said.

"That's incredible."

Nox's hands rested over mine and gently pulled them away from Riker's leg.

Rio snorted. "Yeah, it's probably best for all of us if you stop touching Riker's leg. How about we eat?"

"Yes!" Riker cried, jumping down from the counter. He went around and grabbed some cutlery to take to the table.

It was a very family thing to do.

I glanced down at Riker's leg again. I still couldn't get over how fast he'd healed.

"What about the gunshot?" I asked.

"All better," Riker said, pulling his tee up and off his body.

"Riker," Nox barked, and my eyes were covered.

Riker snorted. "Like Rio, your mate will have to get used to nudity around us. Getting naked is kind of a thing when we shift."

"It's okay. I don't need to see it," I said.

Riker sighed. "I know. It's okay. You're worried you'll like my body better than—"

"Jesus Christ, Riker, quit it," Deacon demanded.

"Boo," Riker mumbled. "Mom, will I be this prickly when I get a mate?"

Ruth turned from the refrigerator with a jug of lemonade. "Probably."

Riker groaned. "Kill me now."

"I will," Nox offered.

"He won't," I countered.

Nox grinned down at me, causing my body to come to life. Honestly, why had I asked to sleep in a different room? I knew where my future and choice led, and it would always point to Nox. I couldn't give him up no matter what I'd heard or learned.

I was 100 percent taken with my stalking, killer boyfriend.

CHAPTER ELEVEN

KIERAN

Why didn't I open my mouth when Nox left me alone in the spare bedroom for the night? A room I didn't want to be in without him in it.

As I paced the floor, I contemplated punching myself for being awkward and not getting those words out.

Dinner had been great, wonderful even. I'd sat back and listened to their lives. Riker was always cheeky. Rio was an amazing cook and kind. He definitely had the gruff bear shifter smitten. Ruth had an abundant amount of information and wasn't shy about sharing it. The three grown men listened to her, did as she asked, like cleaning the table, and they easily showed how much they adored her. Even though Nox was quieter than everyone else and used short responses, I could see he loved being around them. He preferred to watch but rose to the teasing that Riker or Deacon sent his way.

Thankfully, no knives were thrown and no one got shot again.

As I'd sat there, it was hard to believe I was in a house full of shifters, well, besides Rio. If I hadn't seen it with my own eyes, or if someone else had told me of their existence, I would have thought them crazy.

Now I wished I could see them all transform into their animals.

But I got the impression from Nox that he didn't like to be in his tiger's body around others. Riker and Deacon had briefly taunted him over never using his animal in a fight. Since Nox had been sitting close to me with our arms touching, I'd felt him tense, and I worried he would bring out some weapons to use on his brothers. Until Ruth defused the situation by telling them to leave Nox alone. She'd then changed the subject.

If I asked, would Nox tell me why he liked weapons in a fight instead of claws and teeth?

I hoped he would open up to me.

Heck, we'd be talking more now if it wasn't for me, hiding away in this bedroom.

But honestly, I just wanted to be by his side. It was my own fault I wasn't in his room and in bed with him. I was the one who asked for time to sort out my head.

I'd sorted my worries through dinner.

Only he didn't know that, and I didn't speak up.

I stopped pacing to thump my fist against my forehead.

Fool.

Getting tongue tied at the wrong moment had cost me the night with Nox. He'd been so breathtakingly adorable when he'd walked me to my room with his hand in mine and then kissing me on the nose, neck, and temple. He'd whispered a goodnight, and all I'd managed was a noise that sounded like a cat having a fit.

I didn't need any more time to think about my future. I wanted Nox in it—no matter what he'd done in the past or what could happen in the future.

We were fated to be together for a reason, and I wasn't going to give that up for anything.

So what if he murdered people? It wasn't like I had to go along with him and watch or be a part of it. That was his job, and as long as he didn't stalk anyone else but me, all was forgiven.

Nox, like his brothers, was different. They lived alongside humans, but their world had another set of rules that I would one day learn because it meant accepting everything there was to Nox.

Stopping, I faced the door and drew in a deep breath. All I had to do was walk out there, find Nox's room, and tell him I wanted our futures to be together.

Shaking out my hands, I pushed my specs up my nose and glanced at my overnight bag. I'd come back and get it later.

A slip of doubt had me wondering if Nox had changed his mind about me. I'd messed him around by not accepting our bond right away. He could regret who Fate had picked for him.

No. I won't doubt what we have.

Nodding once, I walked to the door and swung it open.

Nox sat on the floor opposite my room. His gaze slowly traveled up my body.

In a blink, he stood before me, cupping my cheeks. "Are you all right? Do you need something? Do you have a fever? You feel hot. What about a drink? Medicine? A cool cloth? Food? What do you need, my mate?" He winced. "Sorry, I mean, Kieran."

My heart pounded against my ribs.

Reaching out, I fisted his tee at his waist. "You. All I need is you."

Heat blazed in his eyes, but he closed them and took a deep breath. Upon opening them, the fire had cooled. "I know I scent arousal, but I need you to be sure. You have parents who—"

"Will be happy for me to have found my other half. The man who will accept me as I am. Flaws and all. The man who will, hopefully, take me to bed and make love to me as he claims—"

His lips slammed down to mine, and I opened to him instantly. Our tongues danced. We licked, sucked, and nipped at one another. It wasn't enough. I needed more. *We* needed more.

Nox's hands palmed my bottom, and he lifted me with ease. I wrapped my arms around his neck, and legs around his waist to grind against him. The heady blast of desire worked its way through me, tearing a moan from me.

Nox lowered my back to the mattress.

I shook my head and blinked in a foggy daze. "Your room, please."

Nox straightened, eyes blazing once more as he stared down at me with a wicked grin. "We are."

"Huh?" I muttered, rising to an elbow. I fixed my frames and looked around. Somehow, we'd gotten to his room while I'd been too distracted to even notice Nox walking.

The room had Nox written all over it. Dark, broody almost. The only light that shined was from an adjoining bathroom. Thankfully, the glow made the room bright enough for me to see everything that was about to happen.

Drawing my gaze back to Nox, I bit my bottom lip when he tugged his tee up and off his body, dropping it to the floor.

"Can you see without your glasses?" There was a slight purr to Nox's low words that spread a tingle through my stomach.

"Yes," I breathed as he undid his jeans and pushed them down his legs, along with his underwear. "You're perfect."

He shook his head. "Not me. You." He moved to the side of the bed that I lay flat on. Reaching down, he removed my glasses and placed them on the bedside table. My sight was a little fuzzy, but I mainly wore them for long distance.

I still had the best view of his muscles flexing as he went back to the end of the bed.

"Kieran."

I followed his hand as he wrapped it around his erection and then gave it one lazy stroke before he ran his palm up his body to stop over his heart.

My pulse raced as I focused on his eyes.

"You're my world, my fated mate. You'll tell me if I'm too rough because I would never want to hurt you."

There was a skip to my heartbeat. The need for him flew higher. I sat up to pull my shirt off. "I'll tell you. I promise."

A purr rolled out of him, but then he shook his head when I rested my back to the bed and started to undo my pants.

"Let me," he ordered.

I scraped my top teeth over my bottom lip as I nodded.

Nox's smile was predatory as he leaned down to glide his hands up over my shins, thighs, hips, and my pant-covered penis. A shiver raked over me.

Nox slipped the button free. Then he unzipped me and hooked his fingers at the waist, revealing my lower half slowly to himself like he was unwrapping a present.

The purr in his chest amped up to a different tune.

When he dropped my clothing to the floor, he was back, hovering over me, and slid his warm, rough hands over my naked skin.

"Please," I begged.

"Anything you want, my mate."

I didn't think I'd enjoy hearing "mate" come from his mouth, but the way he said it with such intensity and sweetness all rolled into one made it sound perfect.

Nox climbed onto the bed between my parted legs and claimed my lips. A moan left me when he nipped at my bottom lip. I gripped his hips and pulled him closer, silently telling him I wanted him inside.

"Soon," he promised, kissing my neck, and then licking down it to my chest. My erection twitched and throbbed when his wet tongue slipped out to trace around my nipple.

"Nox," I cried when he bit down on it before he licked away the sting of pleasure.

I ran my hands over his smooth back, watching his muscles bunch and flex, moving the tattoos that lay there on his warm skin. His ink was beautiful. Like he was.

I lifted my legs, rubbing them against Nox's sides, aching and desperate for attention on my dick. I clutched at him, breathed him in, and drank up the sight of him.

Nox went lower, kissing and licking over my stomach, my hips. More butterflies tingled my insides. I ran my hands over his neck and the tattoos there, relishing in his warmth. He sucked down my cock in one gulp. Moaning, I dug fingers into his flesh as arousal swept down my spine, right to my cock engulfed in his drenched mouth.

Lifting a hand, I bit at my fist when Nox threaded his hands under my ass and pulled my lower half up a little to meet his mouth. My legs dropped wide, and I groaned loudly as Nox's tongue ran over my hole in a wet swipe of pleasure. His tongue pushed and prodded, sucked and spat before I felt a finger tease there.

I heard a pop of a lid and dropped my hand from my face to glance down my body. I drew in a sharp breath, and my pulse kicked up at the erotic image of Nox devouring my hole with his tongue while he used one hand to lube up his fingers.

Dropping my head to the bed, I arched up when his first finger entered.

"Nox, oh God," I yelled, clawing at the sheets.

He kissed and licked my balls. More arousal pumped through me as another finger slipped in, stretching, filling, and running over my prostate, dragging a dirty moan from me.

"Please, Nox. Please. I need you. Want you."

"Take one more finger, my mate. Then you can have my cock."

Nodding, I hummed, but on the next breath, I still begged for it. "Now, give it, please."

He nipped at my thigh, then swiped his wet tongue over it. Another finger stretched me. I pushed down on them, and Nox gave me what I wanted... for now. He fucked them in and out of me. The squelch of the lube sounded around the room along with Nox's heavy breaths and my whimpering.

When I lost his fingers, I lifted my head to watch him give my dick a kiss before he climbed up to kneel between my legs. "Gonna feed my cock into you, *mate*. Gonna bite and claim you."

I nodded. "Yes. God, yes."

Nox grabbed the lube and squirted it over his length, stroking the gel into it while I watched every up-and-down motion. My cock twitched and I squeezed my ass muscles. I hungered to have him inside me already.

"You want this? Me?"

I lifted my gaze to his. "Yes, Nox. I want you as mine so I'm yours."

His upper lips twitched, like he was going to pull it up

in a snarl of desire. Instead, he clenched his jaw as his eyes turned to a deeper gold for a moment before they flashed back to normal. "Good," he growled. "Ours. Forever."

"Forever," I echoed.

"Roll over, mate. Need to mount you, fuck you, claim you, and make you come."

An excited thrill spread through my lower gut and pulled at my balls. I moved one leg around Nox and rolled to my stomach, lifting my bottom in the air.

"Like this?" I asked, with a wiggle.

Another growl tumbled out of him. "Fuck." He nodded. "That's prefect, my mate. Look at your needy hole, waiting for me to fill it with my cock and cum."

Moaning just from his words, I dug my fingers into the sheets and wiggled again. I wanted those things, and I wanted them now.

He grabbed each cheek, kneading them as he shuffled closer between my legs. His palms swept over my cool skin, warming everywhere he touched.

"Nox, need you in me."

"Okay, my mate." I lost a hand but gained his tip brushing against my soaking hole. "You're gonna take all of me, Kieran."

He pushed against me, sliding the head in.

I gasped. "Yes."

"You're gonna take it how I give it, mate."

I nodded. "Please."

His thumbs rubbed gently around my crack when he pushed in further.

"More," I demanded.

"You'll get it. Your hole is sucking me in. Wanting all of me already."

"Yes. All." I rocked back and heard Nox groan when he filled me.

Nox gripped my hips and panted out his breaths. "Christ. You feel good, baby. So good. Fit me like I knew you would."

Whimpering, I nodded some more, unable to find the words as he slowly pulled back out.

"Fuck, baby. Know I'll want to stay in you all the damn time."

He thrust back in, ripping a cry of pleasure out of me. My dick throbbed and leaked, dripping precum over my thighs and sheets.

His cock was made for my ass.

"Harder, Nox. I need to feel you tomorrow even when you aren't in me."

With a snarl, he pounded in and out of me. I gripped the sheets to hold on even when he had his hands latched onto my hips, keeping me still while he used my hole.

Just. The. Way. I. Liked. It.

"Yes, yes, yes," I chanted.

An arm slipped under my chest. He lifted my upper body from the bed and tilted his hips to keep humping me hard and fast. I clutched at his arm, then lifted his hand and sucked on his finger.

He groaned and hissed when I bit down on it.

His teeth grazed over my neck, my shoulder. His tongue flicked out to run up my column and suck on my earlobe.

I squeezed my walls around him when my balls drew up, and a tingle spread through my lower belly.

"Close," I called. "God, Nox."

His mouth slid down, kissing, sucking, and nipping at my skin.

Just as the first shot of my cum landed on the bed, Nox latched his teeth into my shoulder. Stars sparked behind my eyes. More and more cum squirted out as Nox's warmed me from the inside. He groaned low and deep into my skin as he kept coming.

Something foreign yet welcome slithered inside my chest to wrap around my heart and held it in its own gentle cradle.

Nox. The bond. We were mated.

Exhaustion rolled through me.

Nox unlatched his teeth and licked over the mark I knew would be there. I already wanted to show it off proudly, like someone did with a new tattoo they loved.

Except, this mark would never fade, and it would always show the connection Nox and I had. It was on such a different level than a normal human relationship.

My stomach fluttered.

Nox pulled out of me but still supported my weight. He kissed my shoulder before lowering me to the bed.

"I've made a mess," I complained tiredly, but I didn't move.

Nox dipped down and kissed my back. "Wait here," he ordered.

Laughing, I told him, "I don't think I can move even if I tried."

His chuckle was all satisfaction. He climbed off the

bed and went into the adjoining bathroom. I heard water being run as I closed my eyes.

A gasp escaped me when I was picked up from the mattress. He carried me into the bathroom and straight into the shower. There, while my heart melted, he quickly washed me, dried me, and then wrapped the towel around my waist before he sat me on the counter.

"Wait here, please," he said, pressing his hands into my thighs. He started back for the bedroom.

"Nox?" When he turned, I smiled. "You're amazing, you know that, right?"

My lips parted in utter shock seeing the blush coating his cheeks before he walked out.

Had no lover before me given him a compliment?

I would have to offer them more often. At least I had a lot of time to make that happen.

Would his tiger like praise too?

It amazed me how Nox was Fluffy. I wanted to ask more questions about the shift and such, but that could wait. Right now, I was wondering what Nox could be doing that was taking him so long.

Finally, he popped back into the bathroom. As I went to jump down, my foot hooked on the bathmat, and if Nox hadn't dove for me, I would have smashed my head into the glass of the shower.

Looking down at Nox under me, who had twisted us in midair, I grinned. "Thank you."

He glared, sighed, and dropped his head back to the tiles.

An abrupt laugh left me before I told him, "Just remember you claimed me already. No take backs."

He snorted, lips twitching. "I'll always protect you from your own coordination."

"I know," I told him, grinning like a lovesick fool.

Nox stood with me in his arms and walked us back to the bedroom after switching off the bathroom light. It left the lamp on his night table shining, and that's how I saw two bottles of water and clean sheets waiting for us.

I hooked my arm around his shoulders and kissed his cheek. "You're the best."

A new blush rose. Seeing Nox's cheeks pinking was going to become a favorite game of mine.

He placed me on the bed, pulling the sheet over me before walking around to the other side. As soon as he was under the blankets, I was in his arms.

"You've made me a very happy man, Kieran Higgins," he said, kissing my forehead as he reached up to switch off the light.

With a relaxed body and a buzz of happiness inside my belly, I rested my head on his chest.

"It's the other way, Nox. You've made me the happiest man."

His fingers grazed over the mark on my shoulder. "Sleep, my sweet mate."

Smiling, I kissed Nox's chest and rested down there again. I listened to the content purr as his hand drifted up and down my back, lulling me into the most relaxed sleep I'd ever had.

CHAPTER TWELVE

A hum of happiness swept through my body when I woke with my mate in my arms. Unconsciously, I already had a purr going and knew it was from the tiger's satisfaction of having our mate claimed.

We didn't want anyone else thinking they could touch him.

Shifters would scent me all over him from the mark. It was the same with vampires or fae. The only other species I had to worry about was humans.

I'll kill them if they touch him. I'll kill them if—

Kieran shifted and rubbed his face against my chest. A soft mew left his lips, and our purr turned into a comforting one.

A melty and gooey sensation traveled through my gut as I looked down to see his face tipped up toward mine.

He still had his eyes closed with his lips slightly parted and hair a mess.

He was adorable.

Fuck it, I could be honest with myself. My mate looked sinfully hot. With or without his glasses.

My cock thickened with a dull throb.

I needed inside him again. Shooting my load within, coating his insides with my cum's scent. The way his walls strangled my cock had been an eyes-rolling, seeing-Jesus moment and, hell, even my toes had curled.

He was probably sore, though. I didn't want to hurt him.

Yet, he liked how we'd fucked. I hadn't been so gentle then and he'd begged for more.

Grinning at how perfect my mate was, I scooted my hand down to cup his ass cheek.

Another soft mew slipped from his mouth and my breath caught.

How was I going to concentrate on work when I had Kieran in my life now?

Shit, no wonder Deacon did most of his hours at home to be around Rio. The only time he went into the office was when Rio was at cooking school. Other than that, they spent every other waking and sleeping hour together.

A thought rolled through me, but I couldn't possibly see it working.

I was sure Kieran would have a problem with it too.

But I'd at least be around him.

I'd have to speak with the dean of the college first.

"What are you thinking so hard about?" a sleepy voice asked.

Smiling, I tipped my head down, kissed his nose, and told him honestly, "That I need to talk to your boss to see if he or she minds having someone extra in your class. Only I won't be a student. I'll have my own computer to complete work on."

His warm breath washed over me when he abruptly laughed. He slapped my chest in mirth. "You were not thinking that."

I stared down at him. "I was."

His brows shot high. "Seriously?"

"Yes."

Kieran got to his elbow to look down at me. "Nox," he said softly, and I could tell he found what I said sweet but also unbelievable. "The dean won't allow that, and why would you want to spend your time in a classroom with hormonal teens?"

Hormonal teens who probably had fantasies about a teacher-student scenario in their heads. Fantasies about *my* mate.

I had to see for myself if they stared at him longingly.

If they did, I'd soon knock some sense into them since I knew Kieran would frown on me murdering his students.

"I'm not sure if I want to know where your thoughts have gone," Kieran commented as he brushed a finger between my pinched brows.

They smoothed out until I asked, "Have any of your students asked for special attention?"

He rolled to his back while he laughed his ass off.

"Kieran, I'm serious. I want their names."

He slapped at me while he kept snickering.

"Shh," he got out through bouts of laughs. "Oh God, my stomach hurts." He covered his gut with both hands and snorted. "You're adorable."

I huffed. I'd never been called that before. Though, my chest puffed up in pride that my mate thought of me like that.

Lying half on him, I leaned down and kissed his laughter away. His arms wound around my neck, hugging me tightly. I nipped and sucked on his tongue in between kissing and tasting his mouth.

He made a needy sound in the back of his throat.

Pulling away, I smiled softly down at him, brushing some of his dark hair off his forehead.

"You know," he started, "I wish I'd met you a long time ago. It would have made high school better."

"It was hard?"

He shrugged. "Just teasing, like kids do."

"Add them to the list of your students who want extra attention from you."

His teeth flashed in his wide grin. "You're good for my ego."

"I can make them pay for hurting you, Kieran. I would tear the world apart to—" His hand covered my mouth.

"I don't need you to. The past is the past, and it's led me to where I am today. All I need is you in my future for me to forget the mean kids."

When he removed his hand, I told him, "You have me." Even though he already knew.

"I do." He graced me with another warm smile. Although, it turned wicked when he hooked a leg up and over my hip to rock into me. "I would also like you inside me."

"I would give—" I stilled when my ear picked up the footsteps. Sighing, I dropped my head to his shoulder.

"What is it?" he asked, running his fingers over my back.

"An annoying brother and brother-in-law."

"The professor isn't in his room, Rio. Means one thing."

"Riker, don't say it—"

"He's getting dicked and claimed."

Kieran covered his mouth to stop the laugh even though his cheeks flush.

I'm going to kill my brother.

There was a sigh before a tentative knock landed on the door. "Breakfast," Rio called.

"Why aren't you opening the door?" Riker asked.

"To be polite. Not everyone wants people barging in."

"I don't care," Riker told Rio.

"You would if you had your mate in there and he was, you know...."

"I think I know. I just can't understand why you can't say my mate would be fucking me like I was his naughty boy who needed to be punished."

"We can hear you," I yelled, hoping Riker would shut the fuck up and move on.

The door swung open.

Christ, I should have locked it.

"Morning," Riker sang.

"It wasn't an invitation to come in, Riker," I snarled.

"Morning," Kieran replied, and I scowled down at him. Didn't he know giving Riker any encouragement was interpreted as approval? Which was why he skipped over to the bed to kneel there and bounce up and down.

"Out," I snarled darkly after I covered Kieran's body with more of my own so Riker couldn't lay eyes on my mate's naked skin.

"We're family. I'm not gonna take your fated, Nox."

"Riker, I'll go get Deacon and Ruth," Rio warned.

"Yay, family meeting. Then Kieran can tell all of us how you failed in bed, pussycat."

Kieran slapped his arms around me to hold me tight, saving Riker's life.

"Riker, can you please leave so we can get out of bed for breakfast?" Kieran asked nicely. I closed my eyes to calm my breathing while I pictured all the ways I would murder him.

"Anything for you, bro." He bounced off.

"Anything?" Kieran asked, stalling Riker. Opening my eyes, I quirked a brow at him. He smiled reassuringly.

"Yeah, course. You're putting up with Nox. You'll need help."

"Then I'd like for you to please quit teasing him when you're bored and want a fight."

My mate was a pure fucking genius. In just a couple of days, he had a clear understanding of Riker.

Grinning, I glanced over my shoulder to see Riker scowling.

"Boo, professor, you take all my fun away."

Rio chuckled. "Come on, Riker. Let's leave so they

can get ready, and we'll think of something else to keep you entertained."

"Not porn. Tried it. I need the real—"

"Riker, there is no way I would have suggested that to begin with. Jesus." Rio grabbed Riker's arm and dragged him out of the room, closing the door after him.

Instead of hovering over Kieran, I slipped off, lay alongside him, and asked, "How'd you know?"

He shrugged. "It's a clear sign his mind runs a mile a minute, and it's mixed with ADHD. He gets bored easily. I bet the only time he's almost in his element is for, um, work?"

"Correct. He's always been like this. With us one second and not another. He doesn't think when he speaks and nothing interests him, except killing."

"That's when he's in charge then. His mind is locked onto his target, and he won't be satisfied until the job is done. But I can tell by the way he loves his brothers, that he cares a whole lot as well."

"He does." Dipping in, I kissed his temple. "You're fucking smart, *professor.*"

Pink bloomed over his cheeks. "Only on Wednesdays."

Laughing, I flicked the sheet off him and ran my gaze down his lean, firm body. My attention locked on to his hard cock resting against his stomach.

"Nox, we have to get to breakfast," he reminded me.

"Soon." I slipped down the mattress and shoved his legs apart.

"But I have to get to work too." His breathing turned unsteady.

I lapped at his balls in front of me.

"I'll get you there and I'll have that talk with the dean—"

"Nox, you can't."

"I can."

"We'll talk about this later." He tried to sit but gave up when I sucked his cock all the way down and he released a gurgle of desire.

"You're gonna let me have my breakfast first, and then I'll get you fed before heading to work, yeah?"

"Oh, um, okay. If we have time."

"Baby, let me drink your cum so we can get."

"S-Sure." His stammer and the way he bit his lip afterward were goddamn cute. He added in a nod before he slumped back onto the bed.

Christ, my mate was already an addiction I was looking forward to having all the time.

CHAPTER THIRTEEN

KIERAN

scowling face peered through the door window of my lecture room. It hadn't been the first time over the last few weeks, and I was sure it wouldn't be the last. Well, unless the email I waited on had arrived on my private computer at home.

"Professor, your boyfriend is back."

Nodding, I walked over to the door and pulled the blind down. "He can wait the last two minutes of class."

"Or you could let us get out of here early?" someone called.

Really, there was no point in continuing. "Read chapters eleven and twelve before Monday, please."

They groaned as they packed up, but I knew that most of them would have it done.

Smiling, I walked back to my desk to get my own

things and managed the trip without any accidents. I still have slip-ups in coordination, but I hadn't hurt myself since Nox was always around. He protected me each and every time.

He hadn't only helped me in that area. Even though it had only been a few weeks since we bonded, I had a newfound confidence. I didn't shy away from making eye contact. I was still uncoordinated, so much so that Nox worried all the time, which was why I had my own security detail sitting at the back of the room since I refused to allow Nox to ask the dean about working inside my lecture room.

Thankfully, Phil, my guard, blended in. Being close in age to my students helped. What also helped him get the job was that he wasn't only trained in combat but first-aid too.

Not that I felt I needed someone around me all the time. But Ruth talked me into accepting Phil during the hours I wasn't around Nox to ease his and his animal's worries.

At least Phil got paid well for sitting around all day.

Though, that would change soon. Well, that was if the e-mail finally arrived.

Phil walked down the row of chairs as I started for the door. "Good class today," he said like always.

Smiling, I asked, "Did you get Saana's number?"

He held out a piece of paper with a grin. Phil was a human, and he'd been vying for Saana's attention since he started working as my bodyguard. I'd asked Nox when I'd finally agreed to have someone, if Phil knew about shifters. He didn't. Nox then told me that he and his brothers employed a lot of humans for their businesses since they mostly dealt with other humans within the industry.

I couldn't believe they owned so many businesses, and all was run out of one building. They controlled a security firm, a shopping complex, a couple of real estate agencies, a mining company, and then they did the work for their council too.

I hated the thought of Nox worrying about me on top of his own work. So that was another reason I agreed to have Phil.

My guard and I walked out of the room together and saw a glaring Nox leaning against the opposite wall.

Phil gulped and tipped his head down. "Sir."

Nox grunted, and Phil swiftly left with a quick goodbye.

Shaking my head, I smiled and walked over to him. Leaning into his crossed arms, I said, "You really have to stop scaring people."

"Why?"

I opened my mouth, only to close it when I realized I didn't have an answer. "Um, it's not nice."

"I'm not nice."

Snorting, I said, "You are to me."

He growled as he smirked. "Only you." His arm wrapped around my waist to lead us outside. "Are you sure you want to do this today?"

"Yep." I didn't see a reason to hold off telling my parents about everything. I wanted them to get to know Nox on the deeper level so they could accept our relationship faster. I knew they would. They loved me and had always wanted me happy.

The only concern I had was how badly they'd freak out.

"So you see, Nox and I are bonded. I'm his fated mate, and our lives are connected in a deeper way than any human relationship is."

Dad's lips twitched. "Because he's a shifter and can change into a tiger."

"Yes." I nodded.

Mom glanced at Dad with worry clear in her gaze before she looked back to me. "Honey, are you pranking us? Please be pranking us because if you're not, I'm going to get you to pee in a sample jar to test for drugs."

I jerked my head back. "Why do you have sample jars at home?" I waved it away. "No, that doesn't matter right now. There's one way for you to believe me." I turned to Nox, who was sitting close to me on the couch opposite my parents with his arm around my shoulders. "Can you please show them?"

He dipped his chin, kissed my nose, and said, "Of course."

I expected him to stand and shift, but instead, he held out his hand as his nails grew and sharpened. Fur sprouted over his knuckles. A low growl rumbled through his chest. Mom gasped when his canines lengthening to a razor-tip edge while his other teeth went to razer-tip points.

Why wouldn't he fully change, though?

It reminded me that I hadn't brought up questions to him about his animal.

Dad yelled, "What the fuck!"

"Um, so this is only a partial shift. He'd have to get naked for a full one, but—"

"I don't mind," Mom blurted, cheeks pinking.

"Da fuck, Babs?" Dad barked.

A nervous giggle left her. "Not that I want to see your guy naked, Kieran. But... well, I wouldn't mind seeing a real-life tiger in my living room." Another giggle left her. It sounded slightly crazed.

Dad huffed, crossing his arms over his chest. "I suppose I get where your mother is coming from." He waved a hand at Nox. "All this could be is some parlor tricks."

"Are you kidding me?" I snapped. I ground my teeth together and turned to Nox, who was back to his human self. "Can I speak with you a moment in private?" We stood and, as we walked toward the hall, I told my parents, "*If* he decides to do it, he's not changing in front of you both. *If* he doesn't want to, you'll accept that, and I'll bring his brother here who will."

Nox growled at that.

Dad chuckled. "Is he the same as Nox?"

"No. Riker is a fox and Deacon is a bear."

"Fuck off," Dad said with a laugh, and for the first time, I wanted to harm him. As I dragged Nox into a bedroom, I took a deep breath and reminded myself that this was all fantastical for them. They had to have time and proof for it to sink in. I could have shown them my mating mark, but they'd probably think it was just some kink.

I led Nox over to the bed and pushed him to sit down while I stood between his legs.

"I'm going to hit you with a hard question, and I understand if you don't want to tell me right now because it's probably not the right time. We can come back to it at another time in our lives."

He smirked as he wound his hands around to the backs of my thighs. "Okay, my mate. Ask me, and I'll see if I answer."

"Do you have, um, some type of conflict with your tiger?"

His upper lips rose in a silent snarl when he said, "Don't call the tiger mine."

I hummed under my breath and nodded. "That answers my question."

Did I dare ask why?

Nox drew in a breath and rested his forehead to my stomach. "I didn't mean to snap at you."

I cradled his head to me. "I know."

Silence stretched for a moment.

His hands slid up to my bottom, then hips where he lifted me to sit astride his legs. I pushed my frames up and cocked my head to the side.

"You haven't asked me why I hate the animal."

"I wasn't sure if I could. It seems like a touchy subject."

"Only you can, Kieran."

Resting my palms to the sides of his neck, I asked, "Why, Nox?"

His jaw clenched, and he glanced off to the side before meeting my gaze again. "You know we had it hard growing up." I nodded. "What you don't know was how hard. Deacon had it slightly better than me, Riker had it worse, but what I went through was bad enough to scar me in ways.... Well, you know the outcome. You know the job I enjoy doing. What led me to a point where I needed to hunt and kill, not my animal like Deacon and Riker, but *me*, was the lashings upon lashings. The starving, the torture. How I was locked away for weeks with nothing to eat, a bucket to shit and piss in, and no sunlight on my skin. All that time *I* had to deal with everything." He wiped at my cheeks and went on, "The fucking tiger didn't do shit all. It cowered and cringed and whimpered. It was *me* who took all the torture without a reprieve because when I tried to shift, I couldn't. The only time it would come out to help heal was when no one was around. Even then it shook with so much fear, the chains always rattled."

I flung my arms around him to hold him tight and swallowed thickly, trying to rein in the emotions clogging my senses.

With my cheek on his shoulder, I told him softly, "What you went through was horrid, and terrifying, and no one should have to deal with such disgusting, vile abuse like that from anyone, but most importantly from your own family." I sucked in some air and blew it out slowly. "But maybe, my amazing, strong mate, just maybe, the animal, *your* tiger took on the part of you that couldn't handle what was happening. Maybe he knew you held the strength to deal, to fight. *You* were the one who was able to get you both through the ordeal. I think your tiger was the softer side of you that you couldn't show back then. So, in a way, you balance each other out. You're a different combination to Deacon and his bear or Riker and his fox, but you and your tiger *do* work. I'm not saying it'll be a quick fix. You've been pissed at him for so long and I do understand why, but for your own sanity, maybe one day you can accept your animal because he is a part of you, and I care so much about *all* of you."

He'd grown still in my arms, so I didn't know if I'd messed things up by speaking my mind. Still, what I told him was true in my eyes. His tiger was the softer part of him that he didn't want to show anyone. Yet, I got the best of both worlds, because even in his human form, he was a sweetheart to me.

Maybe I had overstepped too soon.

"I'm sorry—"

His arms gave me a brief squeeze. "Don't apologize." He drew in a breath and kissed my bond mark. "I want you to say whatever's on your mind. Always. Don't hold back for me, Kieran. Even if you think it'll upset me or put me in a bad mood. Honesty, all the time with us, yeah?"

"Yes, Nox."

"Good." With the back of my shirt, he pulled me from his chest to capture my gaze. Cupping my cheeks, he said, "Never really thought of it that way. I just held so much fucking anger toward the animal. But maybe you're right. The tiger is chuffing inside me like crazy since you said all that, so I think he agrees with you." He gave me a soft, thin-lipped smile with a shrug. "With time and your help,

I could accept him. But for right now, I think I'd like your parents to meet him."

"You think?" I teased lightly.

He smirked, some of the tension draining from him. "I'm pretty sure. No, I will, and he'd like to scent them as family as well."

Happiness bubbled up and out with a squeal as I hugged him tightly again. "Ignore that sound. It doesn't matter that you wanting to do this makes me feel anything. I just really want to make sure *you* want this."

His hands cupped my bottom and he stood. When he released me, I planted my feet on the floor and looked up at him.

He removed his tee, dipped down, and gave me an innocent kiss before he pulled back, smiling. "I want to."

"Okay then," I whispered.

I believed this would be good for him.

CHAPTER FOURTEEN

KIERAN

With a tiger at my side, I walked back toward the living room with my fingers threaded into his fur at his neck. I smiled down at him as he glanced up at me, still purring, and rubbed against me, almost knocking me into the wall.

Upon seeing Nox's animal, Mom gasped, stood, and slapped her hands to her mouth. Dad jumped up, yelling, "Holy fucking shit!" He pointed. "It's a tiger."

Still smiling, I nodded. "He is a tiger. A very beautiful, amazing one. Like the man himself."

He bumped his head into me before strolling over to the other side of the room.

Mom held out a hesitant hand until Dad tapped it away. "Babs." He then stepped in front of her.

"Dad, he won't hurt either of you. But *I* will if you don't show him some love."

Fluffy huffed back at me, mouth opening, sharp teeth on display as he strolled closer to my parents. I still called Nox's tiger Fluffy, just not aloud since I knew Nox had heard us using it, and he wasn't a fan of the name. Though, maybe I could warm him up to it eventually.

Dad gulped, but Mom grinned and pushed Dad aside to cup Fluffy's face while cooing at him as she brushed her hands over his fur.

Jealously suddenly slapped me in the face and lead filled my stomach.

My tiger turned and let out a chuff. He strolled over to me and rubbed into my stomach, sides, around my back, and then pushed his nose up under my hand as he sat beside me.

He'd scented my jealousy.

Leaning down, I kissed the top of his head. "It's okay. I-I don't know why I felt that when it's only my mom," I whispered.

He licked my face.

Mom and Dad drew closer as Mom let out a laugh. "He's the sweetest thing ever."

"I know," I said with a proud smile, running my hand over his head.

"This is fucking out of this world crazy, but the proof is right here in front of us." Dad shook his head and whistled low. "What else is real then?"

Fluffy suddenly stood with his eyes to the front door, a long, low territorial growl rolled out of him. I may have watched a YouTube channel about different noises tigers made.

"What's going on?" Dad asked.

Fluffy sniffed, and his growl tapered off before his tail started swaying.

A knock sounded. I gasped and pushed at Fluffy toward the hall. "You need to hide," I told him with a grunt since the lug wouldn't budge. "Please move," I begged on a sharp whisper.

Another knock sounded.

Dad ran over there and leaned against it, checking the lock was in place. "Just a minute I'm, ah, naked."

I bugged my eyes out at him.

"What?" he mouthed.

Fluffy chuffed and Mom snorted, but at least she reached out to push at Fluffy's hind to try and get him moving with me.

"Are you trying to get caught?" I demanded.

He huffed and sat his large butt down.

"I swear, I'm going to shave you if you—"

"Kieran, it's Ruth" was called from outside.

My parents stilled and stared at me.

"Ruth?" I questioned in case I heard wrong.

"Yes, dear. Be a gem and open the door for me."

"Who is she?" Mom asked.

"That's Nox's mom. Well, foster mom, and she's also a shifter."

"Huh." Dad stopped holding the door to straighten up before he unlocked and pulled it open.

Ruth smiled as she entered until her gaze dropped to Nox's tiger.

Her eyes instantly welled, and she drew in a shaky breath to exhale, "Nox."

"Ruth, are you okay?" I asked.

She sniffed and nodded but dropped to her knees. As soon as her arms went wide, Fluffy bounded over and tackled her to the ground. Laughing, she hugged him close. His purr was the main noise in the room. Ruth sat, running her hands over him, still sniffing.

More carefree laughter bubbled out of her when Fluffy rubbed into her face before licking it. She smiled wobbly up at me. "Thank you."

"For what?" I asked.

"The last time I saw his tiger was when he was a cub. He's never shifted in front of people until now. Until you helped him accept this lovable kitty."

My heart lodged in my throat. Tears welled. Smiling softly, I nodded.

"I didn't do much—"

"You did." She cupped Fluffy's face and kissed his nose, then asked him, "He really did, hey?"

He chuffed.

Mom moved in close to wrap her arm around my waist while we watched Ruth go through, what seemed to be, something special with her son.

WHILE FLUFFY WENT to the bedroom to shift back to my boyfriend, I sat on the couch with Ruth as my parents took the couch opposite me again.

"I'm sorry for my breakdown," Ruth offered with a watery smirk.

Mom waved her off. "It's fine, and I'm glad you dropped in, so we got to meet you."

"Why did you come here?" Nox asked as he entered the living room.

Ruth stood and hugged him. He patted her on the head. "Ruth."

She snorted and rolled her eyes before we all sat down again with Nox in the middle before saying, "I'm here because I learned from Deacon the two of you were coming to explain our world to your parents, Kieran. I thought I could help."

"Thank you. I appreciate it." I smiled softly.

She took hold of my hand over Nox's lap and squeezed before letting go. "Now, what's been explained?"

"Just about fated mates," I told her.

Ruth nodded. "Right, so nothing about the other species like vampires and fae?"

"Vampires are real?" Mom hollered.

Dad groaned. "Don't tell me they fucking sparkle. Babs dragged me to those damn movies, and they were pure torture to sit through."

Ruth laughed. "They don't sparkle."

"Thank God. What are fae?" Dad asked.

"Elves—"

Dad hooted out a laugh. "Like on the shelves at Christmas time?"

Sighing, I shook my head. "Dad, how about you listen without interrupting."

"Yeah, Drew," Mom added in.

Dad rolled his eyes. "Right, go ahead."

"There are many species that branch off from fae. Some are, like I said, elves, but there are also pixies, brownies, nymphs, banshees, and dryads. I could go on, but we'd be here for a while. However, only a select few have chosen to walk this realm or to travel back and forth through portals. The rest stay in their own dimension, not wanting anything to do with humans. Shifters are born here on Earth, while vampires are either born or made here. We stay hidden from the humans, except for some in government, because all parties think it's easier than being feared and hunted all the time. We protect all kinds, as do vampires and fae. However, like humans, there is evil in the world from all sides. Just know, our kind do our part in helping keep everything safe."

Dad whistled and shook his head. "Honestly, it's a little over our heads right now. What we do know, and can see, is that our son is happy," Dad told them, and Nox tightened his hold around my shoulders. My father went on, "To me, it doesn't matter there are other species out there. We all have hearts. We all have souls, right?" Ruth nodded. "Exactly. Everyone bleeds, so we're all the same in the end anyway."

"And love is love," Mom added. "No matter who or what they are."

Ruth smiled warmly at my parents before she transferred it to me. "You have a wonderful family, Kieran."

Pride had me grinning wide. "I couldn't agree more. And Nox's is pretty amazing as well."

"Thank you, dear."

"I won't lie, though," Dad said, and worry settled inside me over what was going to come out of his mouth after he'd just done so well. "I'm still mind-fucked over all the information and I'll probably have a few shots later, but then I suspect I'll wanna see more of you changing into your animals. That shit is what's amazing."

"Drew," Mom scolded with a slap to his arm. "Sorry, he has no manners sometimes."

When both Nox and Ruth laughed, I relaxed back into my boyfriend's side.

"It's fine," Ruth reassured Mom.

"There is something you need to know, though," Nox said. When he had my parents' attention, he told them, "With Kieran being a fated mate and shifters aging at a slower rate, his aging and appearance will stop around thirty-two. It's how we look younger when we're all older. Our lives can go beyond five hundred years. The oldest on record is eight hundred, and even then, we might have grey hair, but in looks, we'll appear as we were when at thirty-two."

Their mouths dropped open, as did mine.

"I didn't know that... I mean, I... five hundred years?"

Nox tensed.

I quickly added, "Not that I mind. I don't. I get to spend it with you, but it's just a shock."

"Which is understandable," Ruth said.

Nox grunted and leaned in to kiss my temple. "Course

it would be a shock. I should have said something earlier and not assumed that Rio had already covered this."

"He brushed over the aging but didn't go into detail." I laughed, a little hysterically. *Five. Hundred. Years.* Heck, it could be more. That was... crazy.

"This means," Ruth started, and I blinked slowly at her. She was looking at my parents. "That being a family member of a fated pair, it allows us to give you the knowledge of our kind, but also, because we do live a lot longer than humans. We have the chance to offer you an amulet that holds rare fae magic. It'll give you the chance to age just as slowly as your son. With this, though, comes restrictions. You won't be able to stay in this town forever. You'll have to move with us when the time comes and too many people ask questions."

Dad waved the idea off. "Look, Babs and I have been together for what feels like a million years, so I know she won't mind me saying for both of us that there'll come a time when we'll consider the option. But for now, we just wanna keep going as is and enjoy getting to know our son's new man."

Mom nodded. "Yes, that's a decision for another day. We have plenty of time, right?"

Nox smiled, and I caught Ruth's eyes shining as she watched her son.

"We do have time, but we wanted to share the option with you so you can think about it," Nox explained.

"We appreciate it," Mom said. She slapped her hands to her thighs, and asked, "Now, who would like a drink?"

Dad huffed out a short laugh. "I could sure use one."

Ruth stood as Mom did and offered, "I'll help. It was Babs, right?"

"Babette, but I go by Babs. And the husband is Drew. He goes by asshat."

"Hey, that's the best name you've called me yet, honey, so I'll take it." He grinned.

Warmth spread through me. I loved them so damn much. They really were the best parents.

We'd ended up staying for dinner, so it wasn't until we were walking to the car that I remembered to check my e-mails. It was the first thing I did when we walked into my house.

"Where're you running off to?" Nox called as he closed the front door and locked it.

"Wait one moment," I said, sitting at the counter where I'd left my laptop. I really had to connect this email address to my phone, but I hadn't as yet. I only used the school one on there and created this one recently for when I started looking into other options.

I opened it and it sprang to life. I clicked on the e-mails and my breath suddenly caught when I saw the name of the company.

Please, please, please.

I wanted this. It wouldn't only be good for me but Nox as well, so he wouldn't have to worry so much.

Clicking on the message, I scanned the words quickly and started to smile.

"Yes," I yelled, jumping up and turning to my man who stood close. "I got the job," I told him.

He stilled. "What job?"

I released him, fisted his shirt at the front, and peered

up. "If there's room at your office building in the city, I'd like to work from there in my new online teaching position."

His brows shot up. "What?"

"Yep." I nodded. "If there's a room available in your building, I could have my own office close to yours and work when you do from there. We can travel in and home together." When he didn't say anything, fear started to creep in. "Was it the wrong thing for me to do? I understand if it's too much time together—"

"You did this for me?"

I shook my head, but then shrugged. "Well, both of us really. I already told you I was unsettled being at college in a lecture room. This will be something different. Plus, I'll feel more confident being online. I like the idea of being close to you as well." I shrugged again. "I have to finish this semester at the college. And this is only if you're comfortable with the idea of me being so close."

An oomph left me as he swiftly picked me up with his hands to my bottom. I wrapped my legs and arms around him as he headed toward the bedroom, saying, "I'll kick the guy out of the office next to mine and get one of our builders to add a door between them so they're joined. Maybe link the bathroom as well."

Laughing, I shook my head. "You can't kick someone out of their office."

"I can and I fucking will," he said in a tone that told me he didn't want me to argue.

I wouldn't, not now, though maybe later.

Then again, he was one of the bosses.

"I guess you like the idea then?"

His smile was slow, decadent. "Like? Baby, I goddamn love the idea. I'm already picturing all the places I can fuck you."

A purr slipped free when I latched my mouth onto his neck. He stumbled, but of course, he didn't fall like I would have. He slapped a hand to the wall, pushing my back against it.

I hummed, sucking on his skin.

"Christ, Kieran, I could have dropped you."

I kissed on the small hickey forming. "No you wouldn't. You have a cat's reflexes."

He snorted. "Doesn't matter. Don't risk yourself. Wait before sucking and licking anything on me so all the blood doesn't rush to my dick, and I lose all sense."

Laughing, I ran a hand through his hair before pushing my frames up. "I'll try to remember. Now, are you going to take me to bed to show me how much you like the thought of me working close to you?"

He growled, "Fuck yes."

NOX

"Lunch?" Kieran asked as he walked from his office into mine. My body buzzed to life. It was damn good knowing he was only in the next room for his online teaching classes. I could reach him whenever I wanted, and it seemed my need for him hadn't waned even months later. I doubted my craving him ever would leave me.

Leaning back in my office chair, I watched his hips sway as he strutted over to me. With a push, the chair rolled back, and I pulled him onto my lap, where he let out a light laugh.

"I could do lunch," I told him with a grin.

His eyes widened. "Nox, no." He glanced at the door and back to me. It was already locked, so he knew there was no use in fighting this.

He wanted me as much as I wanted him. If not, he wouldn't have worn my toy for him this morning. It was a game we played at least once a week while in the office. The other days were a quick blow job, or a hand job, or a fuck in the bathroom we shared.

Heat hit his cheeks, and he scraped his top teeth over his bottom lip. Fuck he was good at this. Got all my blood pumping to my cock all the damn time.

"All right, but we have to be fast so we can eat before my next class."

Sliding a hand between his legs, I pressed at the butt plug, drawing out a gasp and watching his eyes sparkle with hunger.

"You've been good, wearing this for me all morning, baby."

He nodded, sliding his ass up so he could press it back down on my hand. "I need to come, handsome. *Please.*"

"Stand up and take your pants off. Only your pants and underwear. I'll get my cock ready for you, my mate."

He jumped to his feet and started tilting forward until I grabbed the back of his shirt to stop the momentum so he didn't end up flat on the carpet with a broken nose.

He shot me a cheeky smirk despite my scowl and blew me a kiss before he eagerly removed his pants.

I scooted my chair back further and removed my shirt, knowing my mate liked to see his cum on my skin, and then I undid my pants and pulled my cock free.

"Lean over the desk," I ordered, and saw his shiver from my lower tone.

Kieran gripped his shirt and held it up with one hand

while he rested his elbow on the wood and jutted his ass out for me.

"Fuck, baby. Your needy little hole looks so good with this red plug inside you." I grabbed the end and edged it out slowly. A whimpered moan escaped my sexy mate. My hard and waiting cock twitched.

I sunk the plug back in and Kieran dropped his forehead to the desk. "Nox, please. Need *you* in me."

As I kissed the globe of his ass, I removed the plug, feeling his shudder and hearing the low moan before he uttered my name.

"Christ, baby, you're stunning." I put the plug in my drawer before I picked Kieran up and planted him on my lap, straddling it, facing my way. As my mate slumped into me for a tongue-teasing, hot kiss, I gripped his ass and lift him high enough to get my cock tip at his lubed-up hole.

Slowly, I glided him down my length.

Kieran dropped his head back and breathed out with a sweet smile on his parted lips.

"I'd have my cock in you all the time if I could. Love the way you strangle it in your tight grip."

"Nox," he whimpered as I helped him ride me with my hands to his hips. I set the slow pace even knowing my mate would demand for it to be fast and hard like he loved it every damn time.

His cock peeked out from between his parted shirt. I wrapped a hand around it and groaned when he clenched his ass around me.

"Yes. God, please, yes," he muttered, and it wasn't the first time I was grateful I'd made these offices soundproof. No one was allowed to see or hear Kieran in his aroused state. Especially when he arched back, placing his hands behind him to my knees and fucked himself harder on me.

If he wanted control, he could have it.

For now.

"That's it, baby." I leisurely jerked him off and used my other hand to run up under his shirt to tweak a nipple.

"Yes," he said breathily, slamming down on my cock, squeezing it tighter.

Fuck me, it felt like goddamn heaven. He always did.

A spark started in the base of my spine that connected to my damn balls.

"Shit, close," I warned.

He hummed, watching me through hooded eyes and with a dirty smile.

Christ.

Picking him up, I lay him on the desk and thrust my cock in and out of him, stabbing at his prostate each time. His lips parted, his eyes rolled, and he clawed at me. It only took a few harder thrusts that had him repeating, "There, there, there."

I hauled him into me and sat back on the chair just in time for his cock to release untouched, his cum landing on my chest and abs.

A low, drawn-out moan followed as his walls milked my own cum from my slit and splashed inside him.

Kieran smiled lazily as he patted my chest. "Best one yet," he said with a laugh.

Anytime we were together was the best one yet.

Grinning, I cupped his neck and dragged him in for a kiss. He melted against me until I felt his nose scrunch up. He pulled back and looked down. His fingers glided through his cum, rubbing it into my skin. "I like it on you, but not my shirt."

Laughing, I tapped his nose gently. "Lucky you bring in more."

He rolled his eyes but smiled. "I always have to."

I pinched his chin, tipping his head back, and growled, "And you don't mind at all."

"No," he whispered, gaze fogging over with lust even though he still sat astride my softening cock. He blinked and mock glared. "Don't look at me or talk to me or I'll want you again."

Snorting, I helped him climb off my lap and watched him walk into the bathroom with a grin.

Taking out some wipes from my drawer, I cleaned myself up and straightened my clothes while closely listening to Kieran to make sure he didn't hurt himself.

When I heard a gasp of pain, I called as I stood, "Kieran?"

"All good. I stubbed my toe."

Shaking my head, I rubbed at my chest to calm my fast-beating heart. I'd lost count of how many times over the past six months he'd come close to drastically hurting himself. Thank God I'd been around to protect him.

I always would.

He was my other half. My *better* half.

Kieran had taught me there was more in life than just killing and working. But most of all, he had me accepting the side I'd hated for so long.

My tiger.

He started a purr to show his support, liking what I was about to do.

The door to the bathroom opened and Kieran walked out, tucking his new shirt into his pants.

"You know we love you, Kieran Higgins."

He stopped, head lifting, eyes wide, lips parted.

Smirking, I nodded, stepping around the desk. "Loved you when I first saw you, when I stalked you, and kidnapped you. Need the world to know you accepted me, baby." I dropped to my knees in front of him as tears filled his eyes. "Will you marry me?"

His finger pushed his glasses up his nose as he sniffed and nodded.

"Baby, words."

"Yes," he cried. "Yes, please, forever. Love you." He lunged forward, wrapping his arms around my neck, and hugging me tightly. All too quickly, he pulled away to pepper kisses over my face and neck.

I stuck my nose into his shoulder where my mark was and dragged a deep breath in.

Mine.

No. He was ours.

My tiger roared his happiness.

KIERAN

Rio looked at me for the tenth time and finally placed the mixing bowl down. "What's got you so happy, you're almost vibrating?"

I held out my hand.

"Holy shit!" Rio yelled, grinning big. "He finally did it." Rio walked around the counter to where I sat on the stool and hugged me. "Congratulations, Kieran."

"Thank you."

He pulled away and shook my shoulders a little in excitement before he went back to his bowl of cake mix. "Too bad he and Deacon had to go do that job."

Sighing, I nodded. "I know. But it's their work." I wouldn't ever come between Nox and his job. Even though he told me a couple of days after the claim that I'd calmed the need to hunt for blood, he still felt it important to complete the council's orders.

Rio and I both knew that the people they were ordered to end weren't good ones.

By accident, I'd seen some files on the people they'd targeted. They'd been worse than I imagined. People who sold women and children. Ones who kidnapped men to hunt them down for sport. Others who made men, women, and children do horrid, vile things that no one should.

It'd taken me a while to get over seeing those pictures. But I had a better understanding of their work.

"True." Rio nodded.

Riker ran into the room. "Time to go," he sang.

I jolted. "Go?"

"Where?" Rio asked as he looked down at the bowl.

"Mom and Grey asked for me to bring you two out."

"At this time?" I glanced to the clock on the wall. "It's nine."

"Yep." He popped the *p*, walked over to me, and placed a hand on my back. I stood when he gently ushered me up.

"But I'm baking," Rio stated the obvious.

"You can finish them when we get back. Come on, come on." He went around the counter, got Rio to drop the wooden spoon, picked up the bowl, and shoved it in the refrigerator. He took Rio's hand and led him around to me where he grabbed my hand as well. Together, Riker walked us out to the car in the garage.

"Maybe we should call the guys," I whispered.

Rio took his phone out, but it was snatched away, and Rio cried, "Hey!"

"No phones." Riker assisted us into the car like we were children and got into the driver seat.

"Riker, where are we going to meet them?" I asked, leaning forward.

"Someplace close." He grinned. He backed out, turned, and started driving.

The hairs on the back of my neck stood, and I glanced to Rio who looked back at me, mirroring my worry and confusion in our drawn brows.

"I heard you told Rio the great news, professor." He shoved Rio in the shoulder. "Isn't it cool? We're all gonna be one big happy family. Now, all I have to do is find my fated mate and things'll be perfect. I just wish he'd hurry up and show."

"What happens if it's a woman?" Rio asked.

His nose screwed up. "No offense to women and their

vaginas, but I'm completely all about dick. In my mouth, in my hand, in my—"

"We get it," I told him, face flushing.

He glanced in the rearview mirror and cackled. "Too cute. You know you did good for my bro. He hated his pussy cat and refused to shift, but I've gotten to see his tiger and give it some love *five* times in the past six months. Good things." He nodded.

I'd take the compliment. Though, I had a feeling he was rambling to keep us distracted.

"Thanks, Riker."

"You got it, professor."

Rio cleared his throat. "Riker, are you sure—"

"Oh, lookee here. This is the place." He bounced in his seat as he parked the car and jumped out.

"Rio, I don't know about this," I said.

"Me neither," Rio added. "I doubt Ruth would want to meet us at a club."

"Unless she likes dancing?" I suggested with a shrug.

He hummed. "Maybe."

Riker slapped his hands to the hood, causing us to jump. "Come on, bros-in-law." But he obviously thought we were taking too long. He skipped to our doors and opened them. He took our hands and led us toward the club that had loud music booming out. I glanced up when he gave my hand a squeeze. "Hold tight. Don't want Nox to kill me if you fall on your face."

"I'm not—" I tripped.

Riker laughed as he spun around to catch me with both hands to my waist.

"Whatever," I complained.

Rio moved to the other side of me when Riker took my hand again. He nodded at the bouncer, who returned the gesture as he removed the rope to let us sail through the line. Once in the dancing area, Riker dragged us in close, yelling, "Selfie." He fiddled with his phone for a beat before he took us right up to the bar where he stopped solid with his nose in the air, scenting.

"Riker?" Rio asked.

He sniffed this way and that, then tilted his head to the side before shaking his head.

"Ruth and Grey aren't here, are they, Riker?" I asked.

Over his shoulder, he winked at me. "Nope."

"Fucking hell," Rio said loudly.

"What?" I asked.

"Riker, were you bored at home?" Rio questioned.

Riker waved at the bartender, just as a tall, slim man with long pale hair and dark eyes appeared at Riker's side.

"Sweetheart, you haven't been here for such a long time."

Riker turned to him, and the man tucked some of Riker's hair behind his ear as Riker beamed. "Hey, Soren." He hugged the man, which brought a smile to Soren's lips. My eyes bugged when I saw fang.

It couldn't be.

Could it?

Was Soren a vampire?

Blood decided to pump extra hard and fast through my veins and Soren's gaze rolled to me, then Rio, who looked in shock as well. Had he figured it out too and was on the verge of peeing himself?

Riker moved between Rio and me, placing his arms

around our shoulders. "These are my bros-in-law. This one is Kieran. He belongs to Nox. And this one is Rio. He belongs to Deacon."

Soren groaned, palming his face. "Why would you do this, Riker?"

Riker huffed out a laugh. "I was bored."

Like that explained it all.

"Fuck," Soren snarled. He took out his phone and barked into it, "Close down now!"

Fear barreled into me. "What's going on?"

The music stopped, and an alarm sounded just before other patrons and employees moved toward the exits.

I took Rio's hand and went to go, but the back of my shirt was taken in Riker's hold as he glared at Soren. "Boo, Soren. I didn't even get them to dance, and no one has hit on them yet."

"Let that be a blessing," Soren snapped.

Suddenly, it was only us in the club. Even the bartenders had disappeared on Soren's orders.

The man himself was still here, though. He sat upon the bar, lighting a cigarette.

Riker moved halfway across the dance floor, rocking from one foot to another with an excited gleam to his eyes.

I swung my attention back to where the entrance was when I heard doors rattling. Something shattered and heavy footsteps pounded down the hall.

Deacon entered first, body tense, hands in tight fists at his side while he scowled at Riker. Deacon's shift took only moments, and then there was a bear roaring into the room as he slapped his front paws to the wooden dance floor.

Nox entered, his body taut, and in his hands were a gun and a knife.

"Nox—"

"Don't," Soren warned as he blew out a puff of smoke. "They need this and so does Riker."

Rio sighed and pulled me back to take a seat. "They'll be fine," he said.

I nodded, but I couldn't take the seat next to him. I stood in front of it.

"Riker, I'm going to fucking kill you," Nox warned, pointing the knife his way.

At least he hadn't thrown the blade yet.

Deacon roared again before he and Nox stalked toward their brother.

A gun cocked off to the side.

Everyone stilled when a man in dark jeans, biker boots, and a leather vest over a dark tee walked out from the shadows. In the hand that had tattoos on it was a gun pointed at Deacon's bear.

"Don't fuckin' move," he ordered, gaze wild, breathing heavy.

"Who are you?" Soren called.

The guy ignored him and walked right up to Riker. Deacon took a step. The gun fired, and a chair behind Deacon's bear fell to the floor in a clatter.

"Move again and the next bullet will be in your brain." He wound an arm around Riker's waist and, since the guy was a lot taller, he picked Riker up before moving step by step backward.

The bear growled.

Nox took a step toward them. "You're not taking—"

"Don't ruin my kidnapping, Nox," Riker said with a manic grin. He patted the kidnapper's arm before he waved at us all. "Don't worry about me." He winked. "This must be *fate*."

Well, heck. Riker had just met his fated mate, who was currently kidnapping him for some reason. Then again, he could be human and acting on instinct alone after witnessing a man change into a bear. A bear that looked like he was going to kill Riker.

Sighing, I scrubbed a hand over my face. He'd be okay. And he could take care of himself. I relaxed even more when two large arms wrapped around me.

"Your mates weren't here long. I cleared the place out before anything could happen," Soren told Deacon and Nox.

A naked Deacon, who I quickly looked away from, said, "Thanks, Soren."

Soren nodded, taking another drag of his smoke as he jumped down on the opposite side of the bar. "I'll send the details of that guy's club to you when I go over the footage."

Nox grunted. "Always appreciate the help."

"Anytime. You know this." He pulled a pair of pants from behind the bar and handed them to Deacon before he gave us a salute, and, in a blink, he was gone.

"He's a vampire, right?" Rio asked.

"He is," Deacon replied, picking Rio up over his shoulder and walking toward the exit. Rio laughed and slapped at his bottom.

Teeth grazed over my shoulder, and I shuddered. "Let's go home," Nox said.

Home.

"Please," I said, but I curled my arms around his neck to drag him down for a kiss.

After all, Nox and I had just got engaged, and if they weren't worried about Riker, I wouldn't be either. I knew those shifters could handle themselves.

But most of all, my tiger could handle me.

ACKNOWLEDGMENTS

Thank you to my readers for enjoying Deacon and Rio's story to want to read Nox and Kieran. I bet you're waiting for our crazy fox shifter Riker ☺ He and Corbin will be along at the end of April!!

I'd like to also thank my family for their support. Oh, and happy 21st birthday again to our daughter Shayla, you make me feel so old.

As always, the biggest thanks goes to Becky at Hot Tree editing for fitting these books into her schedule, much love hun!

Finding Out (novella)

Black Out

No Way Out

Coming Out (m/m novella)

Out to Find Freedom (standalone related to the Hawks MC)

Hawks MC: Caroline Springs Charter

The Secret's Out

Hiding Out

Down and Out

Living Without

Walkout (novella)

Hear Me Out (m/m)

Break Out (novella)

Fallout

Out of the Blue (standalone related to the Hawks MC: m/m/m)

Out Gamed (standalone related to the Hawks MC: novella)

Hawks MC: Next Generation

Coyote

Ruin (m/m)

Texas

Polished P & P Series (m/m romance)

Wreck Me Forever

Never a Saint

Working Out West

Diamond MC

Country

State (novella)

Death

Romantic Comedies

Making Changes

Making Sense

***

Fumbled Love

Bumbled Love